# VENOM
OF THE
# QUEEN BEE

*For more information, please check out:*
www.PJHoge.com

# VENOM

## OF THE

# QUEEN BEE

### ELEVENTH IN THE PRAIRIE PREACHER SERIES

P J HOGE

iUniverse, Inc.
Bloomington

**VENOM OF THE QUEEN BEE**
**Eleventh in the Prairie Preacher Series**

*iUniverse books may be ordered through booksellers or by contacting:*

*iUniverse*
*1663 Liberty Drive*
*Bloomington, IN 47403*
*www.iuniverse.com*
*1-800-Authors (1-800-288-4677)*

*ISBN: 978-1-4759-4893-6 (sc)*
*ISBN: 978-1-4759-4894-3 (ebk)*

*Printed in the United States of America*

*Library of Congress Control Number: 2012916760*

*iUniverse rev. date: 09/19/2012*

*With thanks to Louise, Terrie and Mike H.*

# 1

Matt Harrington stretched his legs. The slim, thirty-year-old was restlessly waiting for Dr. Samuel's receptionist to call them for their appointment. He wanted to leave, but knew that the upcoming trip would be a huge challenge for Diane.

He walked over to the magazine rack to find something to keep himself occupied. He wasn't surprised that all the magazines and books were dog-eared and worn. He knew how many hours he had sat in this waiting room. He looked over at his fiancée. Diane was a gracious, beautiful girl with a gentle spirit, most of the time. She was a slender five-six with light brown hair, large brown eyes and fine features. The major share of the time, she reminded him of a fawn or a bunny.

Diane Waggoner was in her late twenties and a high school literature teacher. When they first met, Diane was living with her in-laws. Her husband had died after an extensive battle with cancer, leaving her in debt to her in-laws. She moved in with them and continued to teach to pay them back. All seemed normal on the surface.

In private, her father-in-law Earl Waggoner was a cruel and abusive drunk, who had cheated his son out of most of his money. He controlled everything that his wife, Gladys and Diane did. They never managed to please him and carried bruises from their ineptitude.

Matt and Diane met at a mutual friend's wedding and became friends. Matt was waiting for his petition to leave the priesthood. He taught at the public high school on an interim basis while waiting for the papers from Vatican.

Shortly after that, Waggoner went too far. He was drunk and tried to rape Diane. A fight ensued and he threw her down the stairs. She sustained broken ribs, a concussion and a nearly broken neck, but she survived.

The police arrested Waggoner and while he was in jail, he pleaded guilty. Gladys went to Minnesota to live with her sister and Diane stayed with some friends until she could get back on her feet.

The Schroeders, where she stayed, were close friends of Matt's family. The couple saw each other daily and developed a strong devotion to each other. However, it was a stormy relationship. Diane's physical wounds healed, but the psychological damage from the abuse still wielded great power over her.

During her years with the Waggoners, Diane wasn't allowed to communicate with her invalid mother who lived out east. However, she began to have regular phone calls with her mom after she moved to Schroeders. Surprisingly, it was much less than helpful. Within a few months, Diane was heading for a nervous breakdown.

After a stint in the hospital under Dr. Samuel's care, she seemed to be back on an even keel, though somewhat unsteady. She and Matt were moving ahead with their plans to marry. Dr. Samuels had recommended that they didn't rush into it, pointing out that it would take time for them both to adjust to the changes in each of their lives.

Matt found a magazine about wildlife and paged through it. He started to read an article about honeybees. It was vaguely interesting. He read that the drones in a beehive could not sting, but the queen could. She didn't sting to defend the hive; but simply to eliminate another queen. While the poisons injected by her stinger would not likely kill a human, it would still cause a lot of pain and misery. However, it is sufficient to kill a younger queen. They fought to the death.

"Diane and Matt," the receptionist said. "You may go in now."

Matt put the magazine back in the rack and smiled at Diane. He took her hand and they walked into Samuel's office together. Dr. Samuels put the papers down he was holding and motioned for them to take a seat. "Are you all packed for your trip?"

Diane nodded, "I am. I tried to keep it lean because we are going to be moving around a lot."

"Oh?"

"Yes, we're flying into Baltimore." Matt answered, "But we will go to New York, Portland and Boston."

"I guess I just thought you'd be in one place." Samuels said, "Why so much travel?"

"Matt's nephew is getting baptized in Baltimore. Bea, my brother's fiancée, is in New York City with the New York City Ballet. We are going to see her perform there. Then we are going with Randy and Bea to Portland, Maine to see Mom. After that, we are renting a car and driving to Boston to see Matt's family! I packed a pair of jeans and roller skates!"

Samuels chuckled, "Sounds logical! So, is your Mom accepting your schedule now? You said on our last visit that she was very upset about it."

"No," Diane's face fell. "She wants me to come straight out to Portland and just stay with her. She doesn't want to meet Matt because she's convinced it will never last anyway. She disowned Randy after he and Bea became engaged. At first, she just disliked her. Now, she obsessively hates Bea. Mom can't say a decent word about her."

"How do you feel about Bea?"

"I think she is great! We met when she came out to visit her brother, Father Bart, last Thanksgiving. Bart is a dear friend. Matt's folks offered a place for his sisters to stay with them. We all got along great. Bea is sweet, thoughtful and kind . . . . and very good for Randy. I can't think of anyone nicer. Mom deeply resents any time that Randy spends with Bea. That is just the way her world turns."

"How is Randy coping with that? When he was here while you were in-patient, he seemed to be getting the situation with your mom under control," Samuels said.

"He gets upset, but mostly he does well. When Mom said she wouldn't go to their wedding, he said, 'That's fine. Don't! We're still getting married.' Mom had a conniption and disowned him again. He just ignored it and that made her more furious. She has been trying to get me to say something against Bea. She was livid when she found out that I like her!"

"You said you're all going to visit with her?" Samuels probed.

"Yes, for one day. Then Bea and Randy have to go back to work, so Matt and I will be there for another day. Then we're going to Boston.

She had a fit about that, too. She thought I had no need to go visit his family in Boston. I can't please that woman."

"Just remember that, Diane." Dr. Samuels said, "Know that she won't be happy with either you or Randy unless you both give up your lives to take care of her. She has done it before and will do it again. Is she still doing her physical therapy?"

"No. When we first insisted that she did," Diane said. "She got so she could even walk a little. When the therapist said she could probably begin taking her meals with the other patients in the dining room, she quit. She doesn't want to be one of the patients. She says no one understands how the meningitis affected her life except us kids. She thinks that we should take her out of the care facility and have her live with us in a house like when we were kids. We could take care of her and she wouldn't have to be alone."

"What do you think about that?"

"I think she has more brain damage than we know about if she thinks either of us would go back to that life! Honestly, she wasn't happy then either! Neither of us is willing to sacrifice that much for her again. I'm pretty certain I have cleaned her fingernails as much as I have my own! I guess she is right; we are selfish," Diane mumbled.

"That isn't selfish, Diane!" Matt said. "She just wants total control of your lives. I hope you both stick to your guns. You know, if she would get over her attitude, she might be included more in your lives."

"I know," Diane agreed. "Matt has talked frequently about moving her out here to the Merton Retirement Home, but she just hangs up when I mention it. She doesn't want that. Matt's folks, Carl and Mo, were going to come to meet her too, but she just freaked out. Absolutely no way would Loretta Berg entertain a defrocked priest's parents! She was livid. I told Matt to forget it."

"My folks would've gone regardless, but I agreed with Diane. It isn't worth them making the trip from Boston to Portland to listen to a tirade. They have family to see in Boston," Matt said, then he grinned, "Loretta should be grateful. Mom would clobber her!"

Diane giggled, "True enough. I don't think that Carl would tolerate much either!"

"Well, you have my phone number, Diane. Don't be afraid to use it. She's able to manipulate you effectively from 1500 miles away. Don't underestimate what she can do in person," Dr. Samuels pointed out.

"Don't you think that I can stand up to her?"

"You can, but remember she shouldn't be underrated! She drove your father away, and kept him out of your lives for years up until his death. Try to keep your visits on a non-personal plane, if possible. Don't argue with her. Simply leave if she starts in. Once you get upset, she has you right where she wants you," Dr. Samuels said seriously. "She has done it before."

Diane nodded as the tear-filled her eyes. "I don't know how she manages to do it, but she does. Almost every time."

"How have your phone conversations been?"

"Not good," Diane admitted as she took a tissue. "She gets me so upset. Nora has had to intervene a few times."

Dr. Samuels leaned back in his chair, "You didn't tell me that. Why not?"

Diane wiped her tears and then began to shred her tissue in her trembling hands, "I thought I could handle it. I need to see her. After all, she is my mother."

Matt reached over and took the tissue shreds from her hand, "Diane, would it be better if we didn't stay a second day? Just visit with her while Randy and Bea are there?"

Diane snapped viciously at him, "You really don't want to see her, do you?"

"Wow! Where did that come from?" Dr. Samuels probed. "I haven't seen that snappy Diane for a long time."

The usually gentle, mild-mannered Diane started to cry and Matt answered, "She has been back this last week. It seems the closer to her Mom's visit we get, the more I am getting snapped at."

Diane wiped her tears, "I don't mean to, but Mom has been telling me all this stuff."

"What stuff, Diane?" the psychiatrist asked.

"Oh just stuff," Diane buried her face in her hands.

"Diane, you need to tell me."

"Like Matt is untrustworthy and he won't keep his commitment to me anymore than he did to the priesthood. All he wants is sex and to have someone to dominate. It will never workout. He won't want to let me visit with her."

Matt shook his head and gave a deep sigh, "Same old crap."

"Sounds like it to me, Diane." Dr. Samuels agreed. "We have gone over this same territory many times. You know better, don't you?"

"Yes, I do." Diane said, "But somehow she manages to make me doubt everything."

"Good grief," Matt's blue eyes darkened. "After all this time, I can't believe you still doubt me! What can I do to prove that I love you? I just want to get married and have a regular life. No longer having our lives depend on someone else. I can hardly stand it anymore."

"I know," Diane reached out to him. "Things had been going so well between us. I want that, too. I want to be your wife and to start a family, but . . . ."

"But what? Why does it always end with a 'but'?" Matt pulled his hand back from her. "I'm seriously beginning to wonder."

Diane looked at Dr. Samuels, "Why does that happen all the time?"

"Until you finally stand up to your mother; it'll continue to happen. You have to see her. You have to make your stand, in person. If you don't, things will be unlikely to move ahead. For your own mental health, you need to see her and tell her to her face that she cannot continue to meddle in your life. You have to reclaim your life from her!" Dr. Samuels looked back and forth between the couple, "You guys have come so far and handled so much. It has been good to watch how well you have done. However, until this last challenge is faced; you won't be able to move ahead. I would recommend that you do not visit with your mother alone, Diane. Have someone with you who knows how to extricate you from the situation. Once you can handle that without any problem, then you can have a short, one-on-one visit. I worry that if you walk into a situation like that now, you might not be able to handle it."

"Haven't I learned to handle things better?" Diane pleaded. "I mean, I am better than I was, right?"

Dr. Samuels smiled, "Yes, you're much better. But you answer me—do you truly think that you are able to handle it?"

Diane sighed, "No, I just don't want to be like this anymore! I hate it! Why can I be so mean to Matt and not stand up to my Mom?"

"You have to tell me. I don't know. Your Mom has done much more to hurt you than Matt ever thought about. Maybe that's why. Don't you think that you are more afraid of her than of him?"

"I know I am. She is terrible!"

"Diane, what can she do to you?" the psychiatrist asked.

"What do you mean?"

"How can she hurt you? You are an adult with a life, job, home and many friends that she cannot destroy. Randy is the only family you share and he's in your court. What can she do to you?"

"I don't know, but she will find something. She always has." Diane shook her head and started to cry, "I just want her to love me."

"You may have to accept the fact that she'll never love you the way you want. You have to realize that you need to go to the well that gives water. It does you no good to put your pail down a dry well."

Diane stared at him in thought for a few minutes. Then she said, "Makes sense. I should be grateful for what I have, right?"

"I guess so," Dr. Samuels nodded. "How are things with you, Matt?"

"I'm doing okay, but very frustrated. We're supposed to be getting married this summer and have not made plan one. Nothing!" Matt said quietly. "I feel stupid even thinking about it."

A slight frown played across Diane's face, "Why do you say that? You know we have to make some serious decisions first."

Now it was Dr. Samuels who was puzzled. "Which ones are those?"

"Well, like—ah, your job," Diane suggested to Matt.

"I told you that Mr. Palmer said the school board will be offering me a three-year contract when the rest of the contracts come up. They will be renewing yours. Don't you believe that?"

"Of course. Mr. Palmer wouldn't say it otherwise, but maybe I won't renew mine."

Matt was surprised, "I thought you loved teaching. I thought you wanted to renew."

"Oh, I don't know. Something might come up, you know?"

Dr. Samuels interjected, "Diane, what are you unsure about?"

"I don't know. I mean, I love Matt and I want to marry him, but I don't want to make another mistake like I did with Dean. Then what would I do? Mom said it seems like everyone is pushing me into getting married."

"I thought that is what we both wanted! You keep telling me that you want to start a family. We can't wait forever. Of course, getting married is a risk. It is for me, too! What if we don't work out? What would I do? You aren't the only one getting married!" Matt was becoming angry. "How long do we have to wait to be sure?"

Diane was in tears again, "I don't know. I just feel like it is too soon. I have to decide some things on my own."

"Like what things, Diane? Do you want to talk to me alone?" Dr. Samuels asked.

"It isn't necessary," Diane said quietly. "I do okay until I have to make a definite decision. I want very much to be married to Matt, start a family and all that. However, whenever someone asks for anything concrete, I feel like voices in my head are screaming 'No! Not yet'! Maybe after I see Mom that will go away. Maybe it is all the doubts that she plants in my mind. How can I get over that?"

Matt shook his head in despair and then leaned back in the chair. Dr. Samuels thought a minute and then said, "Can we leave everything open until after the trip out East? Diane, you need to resolve the issues with your Mom. Have Randy be with you, but you need to do this. Matt, can you give Diane a timeframe when you need an answer? Will you be okay to give her this time to work things out?"

Matt shrugged, "Of course, but I should know by the time the contracts come up for signing."

Diane frowned, "Why? What else would you do besides sign it? Where else would you be? You love it here."

"I know I do, but if we aren't going to be together, maybe I should move on."

"You are just saying that to scare me, right?"

"No," Matt looked directly into her eyes. "I am not."

Diane turned to Dr. Samuels, "He is being unfair! Tell him."

"That's his decision to make, not mine. You cannot expect him to wait forever, can you?"

"If he loves me, he would."

"If you loved me, you wouldn't ask me to." Matt said matter-of-factly. "I would likely stay right where I am, but I'd be making my decisions for my own life, not including you. Don't you understand? I'm just worn out! We have gone over the same things, time and time again. Something has to change. If you don't want to make a decision, then I will. This is not a threat. It is more of a plea."

Diane wiped her tears and became defiant, "I guess we have the answer then! He wants to be on his own. I should have known! Mom was right!"

"Take a deep breath. He didn't say that. I was right here, and he didn't. You have to start actually listening to what he is saying, rather than trying to fit it in to what your Mom told you. Don't let her do that to you. Calm down," Dr. Samuels said sternly. "Can you try to relax?"

Matt sat up straight, "Dr. Samuels, I'd like to step out. I'll be back in a few minutes. I need some fresh air."

Samuels nodded, "Okay. Maybe Diane and I should talk on our own for a few minutes."

Diane never said a word as Matt went out of the room. Then she wagged her head and said, "He doesn't want me, really. Does he?"

"Oh Diane. He does. You put up those old fences that we chopped down last fall. You can't keep doing that. If you don't want to marry him, say so. If you do, then do it. It isn't really what anyone else is saying; it is your own doubts. Do you bring up the subject of Matt to your Mom? Do you ask her?"

"Not ever. She brings it up. I'd never talk about my decisions with her. In spite of what she says, I know she doesn't have my interests at heart. What can I do to make her quit telling me that stuff?"

"Quit listening. Either change the subject or end the conversation. That is about the only thing I know that will work. Your Mom has her own motives, and you know what they are. You are allowing her to play on your own doubts. You are allowing her words to linger in your consciousness and taint everything that happens. Have you been unhappy very long?"

"No, not really. Only this last week or two. Things were going along very well and I was feeling very positive about everything. When Mom found out our schedule out there, she started in again. I want so much for her to be glad to see me, to meet Matt and be happy for me. I want it so much. Why can't she do that?"

"Apparently she isn't able to, but that's her problem. Don't let it become yours." Dr. Samuels said as Matt came back in. "Matt, do you have Diane's prescriptions and refills for the trip?"

"Yes, but we need to refill the mild tranquilizers."

"Do that, and Diane, take them regularly while you are visiting with your Mom. Matt will keep the strong ones in case you need them.

Okay? It might be worthwhile for you to talk to her psychologists while you are out there. I think it is wise to wait until after this visit to make any firm decisions. However when you get home, you need to decide if you intend to get married or just remain good friends with no hold on each other. Does that sound reasonable?"

Both patients nodded unenthusiastically. Samuels smiled, "I really want things to be the best for both of you! You go and have a good time. We will meet again when you get back, okay?"

Matt parked in front of the drugstore and began to open the car door. "Want me to run in? No point in you getting out in this wind."

They had not spoken since they left the psychiatrist's office. They weren't angry at each other. Dismayed would be more the word. They were both dismayed at the entire situation and themselves.

Diane shook her head, "I'll go in. I need to pick up some shampoo for the trip anyway. You can stay."

Matt took her hand, "Let's go together. I'd love for this appointment to not taint the next week."

"Me, too." Diane agreed, "But it will. We both know that. I feel just awful. I let you down again."

"It isn't a matter of you letting me down. I know how your Mom operates and what she has been doing to you. I should've just kept quiet about things. I let you down." Then he grinned, "Ah, let's just take it as it comes! Sometimes I think we think too hard!"

"You mean you don't think it is serious!" the delicate lady snapped back.

"No. That's not what I said! Please Diane. I don't want to bicker."

Diane looked at Matt, "I did it again, didn't I? You're right. Let's try to enjoy ourselves."

About an hour later, they turned into Schroeder's farmyard where Diane lived. Matt pulled up in front of the house and they looked at the kitchen window. There was five-year-old Clarissa, jumping up and down and waving wildly at them. The door to the mudroom of the white, two-story farmhouse opened and Nora waved for them to come in. "Wonder why Clarissa is still up?" Diane looked concerned, "Something must be going on, huh?"

Matt turned off the car and the couple went into the house. They entered the large, warm family kitchen and Clarissa ran to them with her arms out. Matt picked up the little pajama-clad Sioux Indian girl and gave her a hug, "What's up with you? Aren't you supposed to be in bed now?"

"No, Missus said I could stay up to talk to you about a secret!" Clarissa babbled as she patted both his cheeks. "I have a most specialist thing to talk about! I waited so long, I thought I'd bust!"

"Well, we can't have that!" Matt grinned. "How about I take my coat off? Then you can tell us all about it!"

"Missus said you can have coffee too!" Clarissa giggled. "I bet you can't wait, can you?"

"Did you just want to talk just to Matt or to me?" Diane asked.

"Clarissa has something to ask both of you," Nora explained. "She has been waiting for you to drive in for the last twenty minutes!"

"It must be very important then," Diane smiled at Schroeder's little foster girl. She had come to their family a few months earlier when her parents died in a car accident. Even though she had three brothers and one sister, she had become very close to Diane. Clarissa had never had much in the way of a female role model. She imitated almost everything Diane did.

After they settled with their coffee at the table, Matt asked, "Where is everyone tonight? It seems very quiet."

"The boys and Elton went over to Zach's to work on the new model airplane. The rest are in bed. So Clarissa thought it would be a great time to talk to you alone!" Nora answered.

"What is it, Clarissa? I can hardly wait to hear!" Diane patted Clarissa's hand.

The little girl took a deep breath and began to talk as fast as she could. "We're doing a s'prise cause Mister's having a birthday cake. Us Grey Hawks are gonna be backerized for him that day. Missus says it will make him so happy, he'll cry. That's why we are doing it. So, each of us kids get to pick some Godguys. I told Missus who I wanted the mostest was you guys. The big boys wanted Matt too, but I winned the argerment cause they all know Diane and I are so much like sisters. So I get Matt, too. Okay? So, please say you'll be my Godguys! Okay?"

Matt was grinning from ear to ear, "Do you mean Godparents?"

Clarissa was shaking her head yes, so vigorously she almost lost her balance on the stool. "So, will you?"

"I would be honored, Clarissa. I'd love to be your Godfather," Matt said as he took her onto his lap.

While he was hugging the little girl, he noticed Diane. Both her eyes were filled with tears, her face was pale and she looked terrified. He gave her a slight frown, "That will be okay. Right, Diane?"

"Oh, yes," she said quietly. Then she added without emotion, "It will be wonderful."

Clarissa noticed that Diane's tone and turned around to see her tears. "Oh, I didn't mean to make you cry. I thought you would be so happiest!"

Diane smiled at her and tried to act happy. She took her in her arms, "It is really wonderful! I'm as surprised as Mister will be! You said he will cry too, huh?"

Clarissa worried, "It's supposed to be a happy cry, right Missus?"

"Yes," Nora said. "I think it means alot to Diane and that's why she has tears, right?"

"Yes, Clarissa." Matt said, "So what are the plans?"

"See, we kids are going to go to church and then get backerized and only the Pastors will know the secret, but you guys will and the other Godguys. That is our surprise for him. Do you think he will like it? I mean he is like our new Dad since our other one died, huh? That should make him really, mostest happy. Then we are coming home and having a big dinner. If he cleans his plate, we get birthday cake!"

"That sounds wonderful," Matt smiled. "Are you all getting baptized?"

"Yup, even Jackson. Uncle Bear is thinking he might come out to see us, but he can't know cause about the weather. Diane, Missus said we can pick out twin dresses if you want? You do want, don't you think? We have to look pretty when we curtsey."

"Yes," Diane was pulling herself together. "When we get back from our trip, we'll decide what we are going to wear. Then you will be my Goddaughter!"

"Does that mean that you will? You have to remember to keep it a secret from Mister." Clarissa reiterated with great gravity. "I don't know how I'm going to stand it! I just want to tell him! I have to practice being very quiet at milking time."

"You mustn't tell," Nora said. "It would spoil the surprise."

"I won't Missus. Cross my heart promise, but I want to so much. 'Sides, Clarence and CJ would whack me! I hope it doesn't make him as sad as Diane."

Diane took the little girl on her lap, "I'm not at all sad! I was just very moved that you want me to be your Godmother. I didn't know what to say! I am very, very pleased. Really."

Clarissa patted her cheeks, "Okay. Cause if you don't want to be my Godgirl, I could have just Mr. Matt. I don't want you to be sad."

"I'm not sad, I was just shocked."

Clarissa got a big frown, "You shouldn't do that shock stuff very much. It makes me worried."

Diane hugged her again, "I'm sorry I worried you. I'd love being your Godmother and while we are in Boston, I will look for matching dresses for us. Okay?"

"Will they be soft?"

"Yes, because I know how much you love soft things."

"Okay," the little girl bounced off her lap, "I have to go to bed now. Missus let me stay up to ask you guys special. Right, Missus?"

"That's right," Nora agreed. "Say goodnight and I'll tuck you in."

"No, I will," Diane said as she got up and held out her hand. "Do you want me to?"

Clarissa gave Matt a goodnight kiss and then took Diane's hand. The two went off with Clarissa jabbering all the way. "You remember how I like pink? I think it is most beautifulest."


After they left the room, Nora looked at Matt. "What was that all about? I felt so bad for Clarissa."

Matt shrugged, "It's been a long evening. Diane is having problems with her Mom again."

"I know," Nora patted Matt's hand. "I thought all that was over after last fall, but this last two weeks has been a fright. I wasn't aware that she has been acting that way to you, too. I'm so sorry, Matt."

"I know it is the worry of seeing that woman. I'm sure she is really pleased that Clarissa wants her to be her Godmother. She loves that little girl. Everything is a traumatic thing for her, right now."

"I hope Clarissa bought it that she was just shocked. She really did argue with her brothers to get you guys. They only gave in because they know how much she idolizes Diane."

"Who will be the other sponsors?" Matt asked.

"Andy and Annie will be Clancy's sponsors and Zach and Suzy for Claudia. CJ asked Marty and Greta to be his and Clarence asked Darrell and Jeannie. Clarissa had to wait the longest to ask you guys, so she was really wound up." Nora poured more coffee, "I never imagined Diane would have a problem about it."

"I'm sure she doesn't; but trust me, her mom will."

"I guess I should've warned you guys," Nora worried.

Matt shook his head, "Nora, it wasn't anything you did. Honest. Well, I'd better get home. That old alarm will go off early."

"Aren't you going to tell Diane goodnight?"

Matt sighed, "Yah, I guess I should."

"You know what? I'm going to go check on the girls and tell Diane you're leaving. Okay?" Nora gave him a look, "I think you guys need to talk."

Nora left and Matt picked up the coffee cups from the table. Then he wiped the table and fidgeted around a little but Diane still hadn't appeared. He decided that maybe she didn't want to talk to him and began putting on his coat. As he was buttoning it up, she came in the room, "So you're leaving?"

"No, just waiting for you."

"Didn't look like it. It looks like—"

Then she froze in mid-sentence. Her face fell and she ran to him, "I really messed up again, right?"

Matt reflexively took her in his arms and held her while she started to cry. He tried to console her, but was rather frustrated with her. "Is Clarissa okay now?"

"Yes," Diane wiped her tears, "I felt so bad, Matt. I never wanted to hurt her in a million years. I love that little girl. I can't believe that happened."

"Well, as long as she's okay now. May I ask you something?"

"What? I really don't want to talk about it tonight."

"Forget it then," Matt pulled back. "Let's just say good night. Tomorrow we have to get on the road early to make the plane. I still have packing to do."

Diane took his arm, "No. Please, ask."

"What was it that scared you about being her Godmother? Was it the commitment to her or because she asked us together?"

Diane shrugged, "Both. What if I can't be here for her? What if we aren't together? I hardly can take care of myself these days."

"Look," Matt's tone was serious, "You don't need to be her mother. She has Nora. You can be her Godmother from half way around the world. Many times people share being Godparents with folks they don't even know. They certainly don't have to be married."

"I know. It just seems like it's something else that is pushing us together."

"I would say that I'd back out, except that I'd really like to be her Godparent. If you sincerely don't want to be, let me know. I think we could talk Clarissa into asking Katie. She worships her."

"I see you've thought about it," Diane said accusingly.

"Yes, I have. I don't want her to be short-changed because of your mom. Of course, I would love it if we could do it together. Honey, I really need to get home," he took her in his arms.

Diane kissed him absently and then said, "I'll think about it, but I won't say anything to her until we get home. Okay? Then I'll let you know. Is that fair?"

"I guess it is. The baptism is the nineteenth, so we need to know. Okay?"

"Okay. I love you, Matt. And Clarissa. I really do."

Matt kissed her forehead, "I know, Honey. I know."

Matt put his car away and got his Golden Lab out of the pen in the barn to head toward the house, "Come on Skip. You're always happy. Well I guess not always, but mostly. Huh? Looks like Daddy and you might just be on our own after all." He bent down and ruffled the dog's fur, "You wouldn't mind, would you? You would be happy to be with just Daddy, right?" The dog wagged her tail and licked his face. Matt chuckled, "You crazy dog! I just love you. Daddy better get packed or he will look pretty silly wearing the same clothes for ten days!"

In his small cabin, he lit the fireplace and took out the ironing board. Skipper terrorized the cats, Lucky and Murphy, a few minutes and then curled up in front of the fireplace. The two cats took to jumping off the arm of the sofa on top of each other before they curled up to take a nap. Matt watched them for a few minutes and shook his head.

He had looked forward to getting married to Diane and living in their little cabin for so long. Now, instead of the dream being near fulfillment, it seemed to be much further away. After her breakdown, the relationship with Diane had seemed to be on a steadily improving trend.

Her reaction to Clarissa's request took him by surprise. It seemed that Diane was pulling further away than she had for some time. She only spoke to her mom on the phone. What would it be like when she saw her in person? Would Diane be able to stand up to her? If she didn't, what would she do? The maternal relationship had been devastating to her before. Could she somehow control it now? If her mom had her way, Diane would have nothing at all to do with him or North Dakota. He was sickened by the prospect, but he also had dealt with it enough to know that he was unable to do much about it. As Dr. Samuels said, Diane had to make a stand with her mom or she would never be free from the internal torment. He wondered what control that woman had over her.

Matt got to bed in about an hour and a half, and even though he was tired, he couldn't sleep. Even Skipper became annoyed with his tossing around and moved to the floor. Finally, he fell into a sound sleep just minutes before the alarm went off. He climbed into the shower and drenched himself awake. He was dressed by the time Elton Schroeder drove in to pick him up.

Numbly, he moved to Elton's car with his bags. Thankfully, Elton who was never too far from a coffee pot, handed him a mug of hot coffee. Matt took a big swig and smiled, "God love you, man! I really needed this!"

Elton turned around in the farmyard where Matt lived and out onto the road. He was a short, slight man with a shock of salt and pepper hair. He had bright blue eyes and a big grin, most of the time. "Hope you slept better than my Nora! She was up and down at least five hundred times last night! She made Grandpa's midnight Alzheimer's walks seem downright boring! About two, she finally told me Diane is back on one of her bends again, huh?"

Matt nodded, "That she is. I think it would be better if I just strangled her mother while I'm out East and got it over with."

"You might have to fight Nora for the opportunity. You know, Nora is kind and gentle most the time; but when it comes to Loretta Berg, you'd never know it! She told me that Loretta has been on Diane's case this last week. Do you have any idea what her problem is?"

"No, I don't really. She has been telling her that I am untrustworthy and we are all pushing her into getting married, blah, blah. I have to tell you though, I'm becoming extremely impatient with Diane! Why can't she just tell her mom off the way she does everyone else? You know, she can let us have it without mincing any words. Between you and me Elton, I can't see living like this. I almost went as nutty as Diane last fall. I thought this rollercoaster behavior was over but it looks like it's not. I know she can't help it, but why can't she? Help it, I mean! Why can't our love be enough? I just don't understand. Maybe I'm too close to the situation, or too selfish."

"I don't think you are, what with all the mess that went on last fall. I'm with you. I thought it was past. I guess we have to realize that the craving for a parent's approval is an extremely strong desire."

"Maybe so, but it isn't ever going to happen. She has been so fortunate that Nora has taken her under her wing. Nora has been more of a mom to her than her mom ever was. I know she appreciates that, but she still wants her mom. There's nothing Diane could ever do that would make her mother approve of her."

"We know that, but she is the one that needs to realize it."

"I'm so dreading this trip," Matt admitted. "I hope going out there isn't a mistake."

"No, it isn't." Elton turned off the car and looked at Matt. "This trip is necessary. Not only for Diane but also for you two as a couple. You have to make a decision. You can't continue this way forever. No matter how it ends up, this situation has to come to a head. You planned to go out there for your nephew's baptism, regardless of Diane. That alone is worth the trip. The rest, I guess, really isn't up to us."

"You don't sound very optimistic."

"I didn't mean to sound that way, but you need to know where you're headed. Good or bad. Right? So, if it takes a trip to see the dragon lady; so be it. My hope is that especially with Randy and Bea there, Diane will see her mom for what she is. Okay?"

Matt nodded, "You're right. I'm so lucky that I have a friend like you!"

Elton grinned, "I know. Now, let's go get Diane's bags so we can get you to the airport."

The men went in and Nora was just pouring herself coffee. "Diane will be out in a minute. Her bags are there. She was ready, but then her mom called. She is talking to her now."

Matt studied the slender, dark-haired lady in her fifties. Nora was beautiful, about the same height as her husband and had the demeanor of a good mother, kind and understanding, but no nonsense. Nora hugged Matt, "I told her to talk only a minute. You okay?"

"Yah, tired though."

They were interrupted by ruckus on the staircase. It sounded like a herd of buffalo coming down the stairs. Then Clarissa and her two older brothers trundled into the kitchen. Clarissa ran to give Matt a big hug, "I didn't sleep cause I'm so excited for you to go on the big airplane. Mister said that we can come with to pick you up when you come home when it will be daytime then, but we can't now cause it is dark out and so we couldn't see."

"That's right." Matt chuckled. "Morning boys. Did you get up to tell us goodbye, too?"

"I wanted to tell you not to worry about your pets. I'll take care of them like you asked. CJ is gonna help me. Okay?" Clarence, the eight-year-old said seriously.

"I'm sure I can count on you. You are very reliable."

"Is that good?" CJ, the seven-year-old asked. "Am I that, too?"

"Yes, it is a great thing and you are. How are thing going with all the chickens?"

"Pretty good. The turkeys and ducks are okay, too. I'm anxious for our bunnies to come. We are going to build the rabbit cages as soon as it gets warm outside," CJ explained. "Kevin ordered them for us."

"You are a busy feller."

"Yes, and I am going to help Marty with his new puppy. Did you hear about his new dog? He and Greta got one kind called a Great Dame," CJ explained.

"It is a Great Dane, CJ. A dame is a lady."

CJ giggled, "Oops! Anyway, Marty said it is blue, but it is really gray. I don't think he knows his colors real good, but he is a nice guy. Do you like him?"

"I like him a lot. When did he get his dog?"

"On this Wednesday. It is for both of them, Miss Greta and him. They are going to share and they want me to share, too. Isn't that neat? They said the dog will be as tall as me, but I think they are just funning me. Dogs don't get that big."

"Actually CJ, Great Danes get very large. They are gentle dogs, so you'll like him. What are they going to name it?"

"It is a boy named Bruno cause that is what the people that had him called him. I'll show him to you when you get home. Okay?"

"I look forward to that, CJ." Matt cast a worried glance toward the clock. "How are we for time?"

"Let's take the bags out while Nora calls Diane. We have to get on the road," Elton said.

When the men came back in, Diane was just hugging the kids goodbye. Clarence and CJ told her that they would help Clarissa with the calf chores, since that is what Diane usually did.

"Thank you. I was worried about who'd help her." Then she hugged Clarissa, "You take good care of Sneezy and Happy. Okay? I'll see you soon. I love you guys."

Then she hugged Nora and said seriously, "I'll remember what you said. I love you. You've been so good to me."

In the car, the conversation turned to Marty and Greta's new dog. It seemed like a safe topic and no one was really in the mood to deal with anything else. It was obvious that Diane had been crying when she came out and she blatantly avoided Matt. Matt just shrugged and held the door open for her. About twenty minutes down the road, everyone had used up every anecdote about Great Danes ever heard and quit talking. Diane, who was in the back seat, just sat back and looked out the window. A few minutes later, she could not disguise her sniffles.

Matt handed her a tissue, "You okay?"

"Yes, I'm fine. I'm just tired."

"Don't do well getting up before the crack of dawn?" Elton joked trying to lighten up the situation.

"We all know what's going on," Diane snapped. "Mom gave me hell again and I cried. You all know it. Even the kids."

"Yes, we do," Elton agreed. "You don't have to explain it to us if you don't want. You know that."

"Yah, yah," Diane snarled, "But you want me to."

Elton raised his eyebrows, "Not really. I was hoping we'd have a nice drive to town and talk about how much fun you were going to have on this trip."

Diane put her hands to her face and started to cry anew.

Matt exchanged a look with Elton, but neither of them said anything further. A few minutes later, Matt checked the backseat and told Elton, "I think she fell asleep."

"Maybe just as well. She can wake up and start all over again." Elton held his cup out of Matt, "Could you refill my cup from the thermos?"

Matt took the cup and filled it, "I pray that things go well. Or at least, not bad."

Elton chuckled, "Funny how our criteria for a good turnout changes, huh? First you want your kid to be a valedictorian and you end up just glad they graduated at all"

Matt laughed, "You are nuts!"

"Well, if I didn't start out that way, I would be by now!"

# 2

When they arrived in Bismarck, Diane woke up in a better mood. Matt refilled their coffee from the trusty thermos as they made their way through North Dakota's capital city. It was still early and the traffic was sparse in the hour before daylight. Elton noticed the sun beginning to rise to the East. The sunrise was reflecting off the windows of the capital building and it was a glorious sight. The melting snowdrifts were almost blue and the bare trees were dark, while the windows on the city's only skyscraper shimmered in gold and red across the sleepy city.

Elton pointed, "Look. It's going to be a nice day! The forecast is for it to warm up a bit. Maybe the snow will be all gone by the time you kids get home"

"That'd be nice," Matt chuckled. "You know, I forgot what green looks like!"

"Right now, I'd settle for plain old muddy. I'm tired of snow. You know, this winter of 70-71 wouldn't exactly make the record books one way or the other." Elton stated. "I suppose it'll be nice out East, huh?"

"Nicer, but not exactly summer," Matt explained. "April is always kind of an iffy month. Right, Diane?"

"Yes." Diane answered, "It was really sweet of you to give us a ride to the airport."

"It was," Elton agreed with a grin. "And I expect a fancy souvenir from you!"

Diane giggled, "I've never seen you wear a tee shirt in my life!"

"Who said I wanted a tee shirt? I want a big old lobster!"

"Oh my, you certainly have grand ideas," Diane teased. "We could've come with Matt's family."

"Bet they didn't have a thermos!"

"Probably not. Elton, thank Nora for me and thank you. I'm sorry I'm such a drip."

"Don't mention it. I mean that. Quit being a drip and don't mention it. Okay? Have I got your word, Bonnie?"

"Yes, Clyde. I'll try to keep my grit," Diane promised.

At the baggage drop, Elton insisted, "Now remember, if you get shaky, call me!"

"I will." She gave him a big hug. "I love you."

"You too, kid." Elton shook Matt's hand, "Can you manage or do you want me to help you with the bags?"

"We can get it from here. Thanks," Matt reached out to him.

Elton gave him a big embrace and said in his ear, "You know my number, if you need me. God bless you."

The couple stood outside to wave goodbye as Elton drove off and then started to gather their bags. As they started toward the check-in, Diane put down her bags and turned to give Matt a big hug, "I'm so sorry. I acted horribly this morning."

"Diane, I don't want you to spend all your time apologizing. Okay? Let's just start today over."

She studied him before she smiled, "Okay."

While they were in line at the check-in, Matt's family arrived.

"Oh no, Mo!" Matt's stepdad teased, "It looks like we'll have to take them along after all. We thought we could get away from them, but no such luck!"

"Ah Dad," Matt teased. "It wouldn't be the same without me!"

"I know," the tall, retired FBI agent grinned. "It would be nice."

Maureen Kincaid giggled, "Leapin' Leprechauns! If you two didn't squabble, the Lord would think He wasted time making your mouths!"

Matt scrunched up his face, "What? That doesn't even make sense, Mom!"

"Look Laddie, if you want sense, wait until at least six AM before you talk to me. Did you be gazing upon that glorious sunrise? Wasn't it grand?"

"Yea gads, Matt," Ian Harrington, Matt's brother, explained, "Mom almost catapulted out of the car when she saw it. I never saw anyone get so wound up over the sun coming up."

"It was beautiful," Ruthie chimed in. "Just because you're grumpy before you have a pot of coffee doesn't mean the rest of us are!"

Matt gave his diminutive sister-in-law a kiss and hug, "I knew you'd appreciate it."

"What's that supposed to mean?" Ian grumped. Ian looked like Matt but was shorter and not as thin. "You just bug me, baby brother."

"That must be why you wrecked my comic book!"

"Yours? It was mine and you wrecked it!" Ian retorted.

"Lord in heaven, will you two ever get over it? That was twenty years ago," their Mom laughed. "I hope you never have a real problem!"

"We don't need one," Ian chuckled. "We got you!"

"Carl, will you talk to your stepsons?"

Carl just shrugged, "Did once. It did no good. How many bags did you pack, woman?"

"I have my beauty supplies, you old Coot! Your mirror should be a warning to you that you need a bag of them yourself!"

Carl groaned, "I miss the old, bachelor days!"

"You never had it so good and you know it," Maureen Finn Harrington Kincaid giggled.

"Yes, Dear," Carl rolled his eyes.

A few minutes after six, the family was settling in their seats on the airplane. Coot and Mo sat ahead of Ian and Ruthie while Matt and Diane sat across from them. Diane had been friendly, but not said more than two words to anyone.

Once seated, Matt leaned over and asked, "Do you get nervous about flying?"

"Not at all. I actually quite like it," she answered curtly, and after a second, continued more softly, "I just didn't get enough sleep."

Matt shrugged, "Me either."

Diane just looked at him and began fussing with her seatbelt. He watched her with a combination of irritation and amazement. What she had said was okay, but her manner spoke volumes. She was putting him off, firmly. The problem was that he had no idea what he had done, besides exist, to foster this wrath.

He leaned back in his seat and watched his family. Carl and Mo were bantering good-naturedly and now holding hands. They both looked happy. He loved that. They were still newly-weds, even though they were around sixty. It was easy to tell that they genuinely enjoyed each other.

Then he was drawn to Ian and Ruthie when they laughed over a joke. They had a great relationship. The petite, dark-haired girl with long eyelashes and his brother not only looked good together, they were good together. They had many challenges, but they loved being with each other. When Ian gave Ruthie a kiss, Matt groaned. "I suppose you are going to neck all the way to Minneapolis!"

Ian chuckled, "Just might, and that's a blasted fact!"

Matt crossed his eyes and began rummaging through the seat pocket to find something to look at. Maybe he was too tired also. He was crabbier than usual and crabby enough so he didn't care. Usually, he tried to be nice and cheerful. Right now, he didn't give a damn.

When the plane took off, without thought he reached over and took Diane's hand. She squeezed his and then removed it quickly to pull her jacket around herself. It made him feel foolish, even though no one else saw it. At that instant, he had an overwhelming urge to yell, 'Just what the hell is her problem?'

Then he realized how many times he had asked himself that. How many times had she given him the big chill for unknown reasons? Oh, she always had an excuse, if quizzed. It was her Mom, she was tired or something. He made up his mind; he wasn't going to ask her this time. She couldn't be any more tired than he was. Hell, she had never even asked how he felt. He was fed up. He jammed the magazine back into the seat pocket and put his seat back.

Diane looked at him in shock, "Is something wrong?"

"Everything is just ducky," he snarled.

"Why are you being so testy?"

"No reason at all."

She leaned toward him and said quietly, "I hope you don't plan on being like this the whole trip."

He glared at her, "Ditto."

She jumped back as if she'd been doused in cold water. She started to tear up and he just ignored her. His mind was racing with every filthy rotten curse word he had ever heard, but he remained in stony silence. He closed his eyes and tried to calm down. 'This is no way to act, Matthew. You can't wreck it for everyone else. Settle down,' he berated himself.

He was trying to relax all the while every muscle was tight and ready to pounce. He was trying to clear his mind, but it was raging inside his head. 'Boy, you're determined to be a jackass, aren't you?' Matt told himself. 'Knock it off.'

As he started to compose himself, he was aware that Diane was still sniffling quietly next to him. He looked over at his family. None of them noticed. 'Why would they?' he thought. 'She is crying half the time. Even the kids know that.'

It made him feel awful that he reacted so coldly. Boy, he was a long way from the priest he had been. He would've at least given a parishioner a sympathetic pat on the shoulder. Of course, he had never been in love with them; nor given the cold treatment a thousand times! 'What do I think that I love about her, anyway?'

Then he remembered all the fun they had, how understanding and thoughtful she could be, how he loved cuddling with her. He thought about the night after the Halloween party when she had dressed as Tinkerbell with all that glitter! What a mess that turned out to be! He still found glitter from time to time in the cabin. No, there had been many good times and he did love her.

It was just that this other Diane was in their lives way too often; and he really hated her. Honestly, so did Diane. So, why should he not be there for her while she tried to overcome it. He was beginning to mellow when he felt her hand on his.

He opened his eyes and rubbed his thumb on the back of her hand, "Sorry."

"I deserved it," she said quietly. Then she squeezed his hand and pulled hers back under her jacket.

"Would you like me to get you a blanket?"

"Yes, please."

He reached a pillow and blanket down from the overhead for her and then when he sat down, he readjusted the air overhead. When he turned to ask her if it was blowing on her, he noticed that she was asleep. Her many quick naps made it was obvious that she had taken her tranquilizer. He watched her a minute and then decided that it looked like a good idea. He leaned back in his seat and took a nap, too.

He woke when the stewardess asked if he wanted a snack. He nodded and noticed that Diane was sleeping quite soundly. "I think she'd like to sleep. Could I get a Coke for her in case she's thirsty when she wakes?"

The stewardess brought them each a Coke and the standard bag of honey roasted peanuts. Matt always thought it was funny. He usually counted them and discovered most of the time, he got nine peanuts! He wondered who decided that was the number to stave off starvation! He opened his bag and counted the nuts out into his hand. There were nine. He chuckled.

Diane stirred and he watched her. She mumbled pleas under her breath, "Please no. Don't."

Matt frowned and she did it again. Matt reached over and patted her arm, "Diane, you're having a dream. Everything is okay," he said quietly.

She opened her eyes and tried to get her bearings. He took her hand and smiled, "You're having a bad dream."

"Yah, that happens a lot." She sat up, "Did I say anything?"

"You said no, quietly. Don't worry. No one else heard it." Matt asked, "Did you take your tranquilizer? You seem to be sleeping a lot."

"Yes, I only took one this morning when I got up," she watched his expression and then sighed. "Okay, I didn't give the bottle to you last night. I'm sorry. Here they are. I just hate it when you have to dole them out to me."

"It is just that Samuels doesn't want you to have trouble with them."

Matt took the pills and put them in his carry-on. "Hey, I got a Coke for you."

"That does sound good," She put her seat upright and took a sip from the small plastic glass.

"Your nine peanuts are there, too."

"Nine? Did you count them?" she looked at him with a playful smile.

"Not yours. I counted mine. I got nine."

She giggled, "You are truly weird."

"How many did you get?"

"I don't know. If you want them, you can have them. I want some real food. You know at home, we'd have had a big breakfast by now."

"I know. Let's do that in Minneapolis, okay? Is it a date?"

"You're on."

Matt took her peanuts and opened the bag. He counted them out. "Well, if that don't beat all! You got ten! How do you rate?"

"Just lucky. Help yourself. I would hate to stand between a man and his peanuts!"

Matt laughed, "Wise woman."

She shook her head, "Did you get a nap?"

"Yes, I think I'm more civilized now."

"Good. You were a bit grumpy."

"Diane, you said you have bad dreams a lot. What are they about?"

"I'd rather not talk about it now. Okay?"

"Will you tell me?"

"Later." She looked out the window, "Know what Clarissa said? She reminded me to look for pink soft dresses for us."

"She sure loves pink, doesn't she?"

"Yes and soft stuff. Remind me to go shopping, okay?"

"I will."

Diane finished her Coca Cola while she stared out the window. The sun was rising over the snow-speckled prairies. It was a pretty day. She handed the cup back to Matt, put her tray up and settled back into her seat.

Matt handed the stewardess the empty cups and put his seat back again. Much to his surprise, Diane reached down to move the armrest out of the way. Then she snuggled next to him.

He was pleasantly dumbfounded. He felt her steady breathing into his arm. He moved his arm behind her head and she cuddled closer into his chest. She snuggled and went back to sleep. He closed his eyes and tried to not act like the happiest man in the place. One thing for certain, she was not boring.

They both woke up when the captain clicked on the intercom to tell of the impending landing. They got their things together and waited to leave the plane. Diane took his hand at one point, and gave him a sweet kiss on the cheek, "I love you."

"Me, too."

Breakfast made them even feel better. They checked their new gate and then went to a food carousel. Matt ate pancakes and ham, while Diane wolfed down sausage, hash browns and eggs. Carl teased her, "You almost licked your plate! Were they as good as mine?"

"No," Diane giggled. "Nobody makes better biscuits and sausage gravy than you, except Grandma!"

Carl was pleased, "It's her recipe! I must've made them a million times when I was recuperating at their place."

Diane looked around the table, "Have we all lived at Schroeders one time or another?"

"Yes," Mo nodded. "I believe we have. Saints above! Those folks have had more people live with them than sardines in a can of vinegar brine!"

Ruthie burst out laughing, "I thought you were going to say stars in the sky. It would have sounded nicer!"

"Yes Mom. Goll—maybe we don't think of ourselves as sardines!" Ian pointed out.

"Maybe you didn't, but I bet Nora did; what with all the piles of dirty laundry!"

"Good grief, Mo," Carl frowned. "You get right to the bottom of it!"

"Too old to waste time wading around the edges," Mo laughed.

"You aren't that old. You're younger than me," Carl said.

Everyone laughed and Carl mumbled some sort of profanity under his breath.

It was a fun breakfast and Matt was feeling very positive when he got back on the plane. Maybe she was right; she was too tired. Lord knows, he was. This time when the plane taxied down the runway, Diane reached over and took his hand.

After they were in the air, she pulled the armrest up again and put her seat back. He did the same and she was soon tucked under his arm again. This time, however, she was not tired. She sat quietly for a while and then said, "I wonder if Skippy is in the cabin?"

"No," Matt answered. "Darrell said he was going to let her play with Ranger during the day."

"It's really nice you guys live in the same yard. Darrell and Jeannie are the best friends in the world, aren't they?"

"They are. Did you know they're going to be Clarence's Godparents? Nora said that he asked them."

"Good choice. He spends a lot of time with them. Clarissa told me all about how she had to argue with the boys, because they both wanted you. You are very popular with the kids."

"I like them. I guess they like me too. They also like you."

"I guess so, but I think it's because I'm going with you."

"No. We know better than that."

"I was thinking, we should get you a matching pink shirt!"

"Don't think so."

Diane grinned, "How about a pink necktie?"

"How about no?"

"Chicken."

"Go to sleep."


Allen Adams met the family. After Carl picked up a rental car, the men loaded the bags into the two cars. Allen, Abby's husband, worked at the shipyards and was usually quiet. Around folks he was comfortable with, he could talk up a storm. It was their child, little Austin that was going to be baptized. Abby was fairer than Ian and Matt, but looked a lot like her Mom. They all did. Auburn hair, tanned complexion and big dimples. Allen however, was a tall and lanky fellow with sandy hair.

"My Mom will be here tonight. She is driving down from Annapolis. She wants to get here before dark," Allen said as he helped load the baggage into two cars. "We thought we'd eat at home tonight. Okay? Then we can go out tomorrow night."

"That sounds fine," Carl said. "Whatever you decide. Austin will be baptized tomorrow?"

"Yes, we decided to get it done on Saturday rather than fuss with all the Palm Sunday commotion. You know how that is."

"Yes," Maureen smiled. "What time?"

"I wanted it early in the morning, so we'd have time to go fishing. Then Abby torqued out about that," Allen's eyes twinkled. "She explained that it will be at two o'clock."

Ian chuckled, "I suppose we'd have time to go fishing early in the morning."

"If you are brave enough, I'm fine with it. Your sister likely has a different take on the issue!"

"I bet she does," Ian guffawed. Ruthie whacked him.

Adam's little cottage smelled like a wonderful dinner when the group arrived. Abby greeted them all with big hugs and welcomed them in. "Mr. Austin is still napping, but he'll be up before long."

When she hugged Diane she said, "Oh, your brother called. He asked that you call when you get in."

"Thank you, Abby. I will in a bit, unless it was urgent."

"He didn't say that. I think he just wants to see if you made it."

Their bags were taken to the different areas where cots were made out. Diane and Marta Adams would share the attic bedroom and Ian and Ruthie would have the hide-a-bed in the basement. Carl and Mo had the guest room, but Matt would have to sleep on the sofa.

Matt crossed his eyes, "Thanks, Sis."

She giggled, "I knew you wouldn't mind. And you don't, do you?"

"Would it matter if I did?"

"Not one bit."

"Figured."

While Mo was putting her things away, she tiptoed into the nursery and watched the baby sleep. Mo hadn't seen him before and was very excited. She smiled and cooed until Austin woke up. The happy grandmother picked him out of his crib and gave him a hug. Then she came down stairs proud as punch carrying her newest grandson. "He's a fine one, Abby! You and Allen have a fine Laddie!"

He was six months old, had bright blue eyes and carrot red hair. He was a smiley child and quite active.

"Mo, you just had to wake him up, didn't you?" Carl said as he got up and took the boy from her.

"I just got a bit lost on my way to the stairway!"

"Yah, Mom. We know!" Ruthie giggled. "You woke him up because you couldn't wait."

"Austin wanted to be meeting his Granny, so what was I to do?"

Abby looked at her son, "Did Granny change his diaper too?"

"We got that all taken care of, didn't we Austin?" Mo took his little hand and tickled his cheek. "Isn't he the cutest little thing you ever did see?"

Carl nodded with pride, "Drag out your camera, Mo! I want a photo of me and the little guy to make Elton jealous. That old Magpie always thinks his grandkids are the cutest."

"Yah Dad, and you always think yours are," Matt patted his stepdad on the back.

Carl enjoyed playing with him. Even though he preferred children when they weren't newborn, Carl had become quite adept at handling small children.

The family had a wonderful visit. After a bit, Abby turned to Diane, "I imagine you are all a tither with wedding plans? Have you set a date yet?"

Matt held his breath, but Diane smiled, "Not yet. We've had a busy winter. Schroeder's took in five orphans this winter. Things have been exciting. The oldest is eight and the youngest is a year and a half. They're all from the same family."

"Wow," Allen said, "That is a bunch. How did they come to know them?"

"Remember Andy Schroeder, who was in Vietnam? He and his two best friends were wounded and sent home. One of his buddies, Jackson was from Pine Ridge Indian Reservation. His home life was a shambles, so Schroeder's took him to live with them. After the New Year, his Mom and stepdad died in a car accident. They left five kids. Nora and Elton couldn't see letting the kids be split up, because it would have driven Jackson crazy, so they became foster parents for all of them!" Mo explained. "It has been quite an adventure, but the kids are doing well now."

"If you can't do well living at Schroeders," Diane offered, "There has to be something wrong with you."

"So, they all live where you do?" Allen asked.

"Yes. I have a huge family now. Oh, I forgot to call Randy. May I use your phone?"

"Of course. There is one in the other room if you want some privacy." Allen stood to show her.

"I will pay you."

"No, you won't. You're family. Don't be silly, unless you want to pay for the Coke you just drank too?"

Diane patted her jeans pocket, "Guess I lost my wallet somewhere."

"A likely tale."

Matt barely listened to the conversation at the table while waiting for Diane to return. When she did, she seemed to be in a good mood although a bit more quiet. He was relieved and soon forgot all about it.

Mrs. Adams arrived and they all had a wonderful dinner. That evening, the men went out to the backyard to have a drink and to smoke the cigars that Allen had handed out.

Matt was delighted that things had gone so well that evening. While they were sitting outside, Diane came to the patio and asked Matt if she could see him for a bit. He nodded and went to join her.

"I need your help a minute."

"Sure."

When they were alone, she asked him where the mild tranquilizers were that they had picked up. "I got them in my suitcase. I'll get you one."

"Can't I just keep the bottle? Then I wouldn't have to disturb you."

Matt put his arms around his fiancée and gave her a hug, "You know what Dr. Samuels says. No way. He'd have my hide."

"This is silly. It makes me feel like an addict or something."

"Don't feel like that. Did something happen with Randy?"

"No, Randy just confirmed he'll be here Sunday about one and said Mom is on a real rip, but we knew that. I just don't want to be a burden to everyone."

"Shall we go for a walk? Would you like to talk?"

Diane took the pill, "No. I think I'll be hitting the sack in a little bit. I want to get some sleep tonight so I don't wake up like this morning."

Matt kissed her, "Okay. But if you need to talk, let me know. Promise?"

"Cross my heart," Diane smiled. "Good night."

It was about two when Matt stirred as the light came on in the kitchen. He turned over and tried to cover his head. He heard someone getting a drink of water. A minute or so later, he felt a hand on his shoulder. He turned over and saw Diane. "I'm sorry to bother you, but I need to talk to you."

Matt changed his position to sit up. He had on his old sloppy green tee shirt and his gray sweatpants, and his hair was sticking out in every direction. He yawned and stretched. When his eyes adjusted, he noticed how pretty she was.

Her hair was messy, but she looked so sweet and innocent in her pink pajamas. He grinned, "I bet Clarissa packed those!"

Diane giggled softly, "She did. I wasn't going to bring them, but she said I should. Guess she was right."

"Good choice," Matt said and he put his arms around her. "What is it? Hey, can I have a drink of your water?"

She handed him her water and then said, "I should have done this before, but I have been afraid. You know, I haven't seen Mom in almost five years. We did not part on good terms. She told me she'd make me pay for leaving her."

"Don't you think she was just angry?"

"You don't know Mom. She is cruel and vengeful. More than either you or Dr. Samuels can imagine. Matt, I'm terrified about seeing her."

Matt pulled Diane next to him on the sofa, "Would you rather not see her? We can cancel it if you think that would be best."

"No, I have to. I know I do. Randy said that, too. Matt, she has been awful to Bea. I guess if Bea can still see her, I can."

"If she is horrible then no one should have to see her."

"You don't understand. It is something I have to do, but I'm so afraid I won't be able to stand up to her. She won't be nice to you, even if she makes you think she is being nice."

"I didn't expect she would be nice."

"It's more than that. Every time Randy or I have ever cared about something or someone, Mom has always purposely destroyed it."

"How's that?"

"I can't explain it. She just does it. Matt, what if she drives you away from me?" Then Diane started to cry and Matt put his arms around her.

"She won't. I love you."

"I wish I was as certain as you. In my experience, Mom has always won. I tried ever since Dad left to not let her know what I cared about, so she wouldn't do that. If she even senses that either of us kids are excited or happy about something, she will do it. I think that is why I am so frightened of relaxing and being happy. She will mess it up; one way or the other."

"Honey, what could she do to us?" Matt asked. "We are adults and live far away from her. She can't do anything to us."

"I wish I could believe that. That is why I am so afraid that she will know how much we love each other and how happy I am. It scares me to death."

"My little Tinker, we will be fine. Okay?"

"I hope so."

Mostly they just sat on the sofa and hardly talked at all. He tried to comfort her, even though he wasn't exactly sure what her concern was. Surely, they would be able to handle an invalid.

They dozed off, but when Austin woke up, they did too. Diane said, "I better go back to bed. Matt, no matter how things end up, please always remember that I love you with all my heart."

They kissed and she went upstairs. He lay back down and tried to understand what she meant.

Matt couldn't shake his conversation with Diane. He'd never heard that foreboding in her voice before. It concerned him, but he had nothing concrete to put with it. He knew that Loretta Berg was mean-spirited. Neither Diane nor Randy mentioned she'd ever been physical in any way. In fact, she was an invalid since her bout with meningitis years earlier. It seemed that she barely was capable of movement at all. Matt knew full well that her talk was vicious and that was more than enough for a person bear. However, there seemed to be more in what Diane was trying to say. At least, he was glad that she finally talked to him.

The day was busy and the family had enough things to do to keep his mind occupied. Diane seemed to be having a good time too, and for that, he was thankful.

The baptism was at St. Andrew's ornate chapel and very nice. Little Austin was mesmerized with Father John's heavy cross and got a good grip on it twice! Other than that, he was a well-behaved little boy.

His Aunt Ruthie held him at the font. She really enjoyed it and it seemed he did, too. Diane did not take part, but chose to sit with the grandparents. Matt was not surprised, considering how she reacted to Clarissa, but no one mentioned it. Allen and Abby spoke as if she was the baby's Godmother, but never asked why she didn't stand with Matt.

That evening, Allen and Abby made reservations at a local supper club. Marta, Carl and Mo chose to stay home with Austin, but the young couples went out. They ate in the dining room and then adjourned to the bar area that had a large dance floor. They had a great time.

That night, Matt was wishing that Diane would come down for another drink of water, but decided that it was probably best that she didn't. He knew he'd better get married pretty soon, or he would forget about chastity. He had himself nearly convinced that the 'thou shalt not commit adultery' was a misprint or at least, misinterpreted.

Sunday morning after Mass, the family returned to the cottage to a great ham dinner. Abby had invited Randy to join them. He arrived from the airbase at Dover, Delaware just as they were sitting down to eat.

Randy was six foot tall and had the looks of a movie star. He had brown hair and eyes and a great build. He was very assured as one would expect a lieutenant in the Air Force to be. After he greeted those he knew with big embraces, he introduced himself to the Adam's family.

"It was very nice of you to invite me for dinner." Randy grinned, "You didn't have to, but I'm very glad you did. So, where is the little boy of honor? What's his name, Dallas?"

Allen laughed, "No, Austin. Carl is carrying him around. He's going to have him spoiled rotten."

"Carl's good at that," Randy went to Carl and then held out his hands for the baby, "May I?"

Carl took a judgmental stance, "Do you know anything about holding a baby?"

Randy laughed, "About as much as you do!"

"Doubt that," Carl grumbled.

Randy played with the little boy and then handed him back to Carl. "He sure has a mess of red hair!"

"I know," Allen agreed. "I plan on getting his hair dyed before he starts school! Lordie be, he looks like a carrot!"

After dinner, they packed their cars and said their goodbyes. Marta left for her home and the Harringtons left for Boston. Matt and Diane went with Randy to New York City to see Bea.

"We wanted to see Bea dance, too," Mo explained. "But it seems that the kids planned a big family bash up in Boston tomorrow. So, we'll have to do that at a later time. Please give her our best. We love her to pieces and still have her ballet room ready when she comes to visit."

"She raves about all the fun she had at your house," Randy teased. "Of course, that is when she met me, so I imagine it was more me than Coot."

Carl groused, "Doubt that very much!"

Mo patted Carl's balding head, "We know. Coot Hefner and his women! Really Coot."

# 3

It was late when the three arrived at Bea's small fifth-floor, one-bedroom apartment. She met them at the door with a big hug and welcome. "I was so anxious for you to arrive! I couldn't wait. I made some submarine sandwiches for us. I hope that's okay."

"It's wonderful," Diane said. "I can't wait to see you perform tomorrow night! Remind me, I have to steal a bunch of programs. Everyone has asked me to bring some back!"

"I'll get you some so you don't have to steal," Bea offered and motioned to the small table. "Have a seat. I put out my best china, as you can see!"

Randy laughed, "We are registered at Dixie Cup of America in case you are wondering!"

Matt grinned, "Looks like something I could like. Saves a lot of dishwashing!"

"Have you made your wedding plans yet, Diane?" Bea asked.

Diane shook her head no and made an excuse to run off to the bathroom. It left Matt to answer. Bea looked at him, "Did you set a date?"

"Not yet. No plans," he said and sat down at the table.

Randy watched him and then asked, "Diane?"

Matt nodded and then said, "She thought she'd wait until after she sees Loretta."

Randy huffed and Bea put her arms around Matt's shoulders, "Good luck."

"What's the story? I'm going crazy! Diane is all weird and now you two?"

Randy shook his head, "It's bad, man."

Then Diane came back in the room and the subject was changed.

Bea and Randy made out the futon for the men and then she and Diane went to bed. Diane had taken a tranquilizer before she went to bed, so she slept all night. Matt was awake most the night and wondered if he should take a pill. He almost woke Randy, but decided the poor guy needed his rest. They could talk later.

The next day proved to be busy enough so there was no time to talk to Randy alone. They hardly saw Bea all that day, but they visited many of New York City's sights. That evening, they got ready to go to the ballet at the Lincoln Center.

The performance of the Firebird by Stravinsky was wonderful and Bea did a great job, especially in the Rite of Spring. The sets and costumes were fantastic versions of the fairy tale creatures in the piece. They were all enthralled.

After the performance, they went backstage. Bea introduced them to the lead dancers and the director. It was incredible. Bea went to change and said she would meet them at the side door. Then the four went out on the town.

They had a fine dinner. It was something to remember. "This evening has been magnificent," Diane said. "I can't imagine anything more wonderful. You're a great dancer, Bea."

"Not really, there are many better."

"Not in my book," Randy said with pride. "But then, I'm not in love with them!"

Diane grabbed her heart in mock shock, "I never thought I'd live so long as to hear my very own brother say those words!"

Bea raised her eyebrow, "You mean he didn't leave a bunch of heartbroken women to be by my side?"

"He may have, but he never loved them."

Randy frowned, "I don't know if I like this conversation. Let's talk about Matt."

"Nothing to say. I went from priest to fiancée in a twinkle of the eye."

"I bet there were still a few ladies that were sad about it," Bea suggested. "I know my sister Bonnie was, but that wasn't surprising. Boy, talk about someone changing! Since she started dating Darrell's brother Sammy she doesn't even look at another man! I can't believe the transformation."

Matt laughed, "That's good to know. Sam has become almost domestic since he met Bonnie. Who would have ever guessed?"

"Probably Joey and Beth," Bea giggled. "They are on the phone so much; I can't imagine they get anything else done!"

"When Joey and Sam get hitched, that will be the last of the Jessup boys! I guess Darrell was never a dandy like those two. Jeannie was the apple of his eye forever. The neighborhood won't be the same," Matt chuckled. "They are great guys. Have the two couples decided where their relationships are going?"

"A little bit." Bea answered. "Beth will be graduating in the spring and has already applied for jobs in North Dakota. She is a meteorologist. Being an electrical engineer, Bonnie already has a line on a job at one of the power plants near Sammy. I guess they are talking about a double wedding. That way, Bart can marry them, since his parish is in Merton."

"Have you decided where you are getting married?" Matt asked.

"Merton," Randy answered. "And Father Bart will do the honors. After all, why have a priest for a brother-in-law, if he can't do something for you? We'd like you and Diane to stand up for us."

Diane's eyes widened and she bolted from the room. Bea and Randy were dumbfounded. Matt stood, "Don't worry. I'll go talk to her."

Matt entered the small bedroom but didn't see Diane. He noticed the bathroom door and entered it. Diane was crying and gave him a filthy look. "Excuse me! Don't you knock?"

He had a hard time getting his arms around her because she was resisting, but he finally clenched her inside his embrace. She stood smoldering for a minute and then burst into tears. He held her until she calmed a bit and then handed her a piece of toilet paper to wipe her eyes. Her breathing was hampered by huge intermittent sobs, but she began to get control again.

"It's okay," Matt whispered calmly in her ear. "You're with family. We all love you. Just relax. No need to pretend about anything. Hear me?"

She simply cried more, but Matt could tell she was regaining her strength. After a few minutes, she put her arms around his neck. "Matt, do you think that you could go out there with me? I need to talk to them."

"Want to splash some water on your face?"

"Yes, please."

Matt stayed with her while she ran the cold water into her hands and put it on her face. She was trembling and quite unsteady. When she dried her face, they went out to the other room.

Randy and Bea had made up the futon and set some cups out for tea. "Tea will be ready in a few minutes."

As Diane moved toward the table, Randy took her in his arms. He gave her a hug and said, "It's okay, Sis. You're among friends."

She looked at her brother and whimpered, "Mom said, 'This will be a time of requitement'. Did she tell you that?"

Randy embraced her, "Don't worry. I know. She told me, too. Just remember, she can't do anything! Keep that in your mind. She can't have a time of requitement."

Matt and Bea looked at each other with more questions than answers. Thankfully, the teapot whistled and Bea got up to get it. Matt went to help her.

Matt and Bea silently put the tea bags in the cups and filled them with the hot water. Matt took two to the table and Bea followed with the other two. Before she sat down, she asked, "Sugar, lemon or milk?"

"Sugar please," Diane said and began to sit down.

"For me, too," Matt said as he sat next to Diane.

Randy pulled out the chair for Bea and they all sat stirring their tea. Finally, Matt broke the silence, "What is requitement?"

Randy never looked up. "It is an old word; from requite which means to pay back in kind. You've heard of unrequited love? That means it wasn't paid back in kind. Mom always used it to mean like pay back or retaliation. The word is seldom used nowadays and when it is used mostly as something that is required."

It was a few minutes before Bea said, "I don't understand."

Randy continued, "Mom only uses it as a revenge thing; not payback for something she thought we did nice for her."

Diane added sarcastically, "She never thought we did anything nice for her! Ever."

He shrugged, "That's true."

Matt frowned, "I don't get it. Has she done this all your life? Like what does she do?"

Randy raised his eyebrows, "Only after Dad left, although I'm pretty sure that she did it to him. She does different things depending, but is never good."

"You mean like physical punishment?"

Randy shook his head, "Oh no; well yah, but not like a beating. She was quite weak after the meningitis; so she couldn't do much physically. She makes you pay in ways you can't even imagine. She usually wrecks or destroys something you really care about."

Bea took Randy's hand, "Look, you have to tell us. Matt and I deserve to know. Not only for yourselves, but for us. I know she has said hateful, rude things to me, but I also know that you'd never get that bent out of shape about that stuff. Ever since your last talk with her, you've been acting like you were sentenced to the guillotine."

"I'm sorry," Randy took her hand. "I know. It isn't fair to you. I just don't know what to warn you about, because with her you never know. She is cruel and twisted."

"Maybe it'd be wise to call her psychiatrist and see if a trip is even advisable. I see no point in traveling all that way for her to hurt you guys," Matt pointed out. "Diane has been a mess for almost two weeks now. I don't want her to have to go through this."

"Don't you understand?" Diane took his arm, "If I don't go and face her, I'll never get past this. You know what Dr. Samuels said."

"Did you tell him about this requite thing? I never heard it before."

"I mentioned it when I was in the hospital, but I didn't tell him lately. It wouldn't change his mind anyway. Remember, he told me that maybe I take all this mess out on you because you are less scary than her? Well, you are less scary. I have to face it."

"What kind of stuff does she do? What can she do to you?"

Randy leaned back, "When I wanted to go out for the track team in junior high, Mom was against it. She told me no, but I signed up anyway. Unbeknownst to me, the coach called her and asked if she would sign the permission slip. She said yes and acted as sweet as pie. That morning before the first tryouts, she made some brownies with chocolate frosting on them. She told me to eat them on the way to school, so that I'd have extra energy for the tryouts. I actually thought she had come around and was okay with it. I started to feel stomach cramps before the race, but I ran it anyway. I got explosive diarrhea and not only couldn't compete, was totally embarrassed in front of the whole team. When I got home, she laughed. She asked how I liked my requitement."

Bea's mouth fell open, "Randy, did she poison you?"

"Not really, but sort of. She frosted the brownies with chocolate-flavored laxative." Randy looked at Diane with tears in his eyes, "I never tried that again, did I?"

"No, you didn't. Look how long it took my hair to grow back when I decided to cut my hair!"

Bea frowned, "What happened?"

"I wanted this new haircut and Mom said that we couldn't afford it. I took some extra babysitting jobs and got the haircut. She was furious. That night, she was very sweet and said, 'You know, I really like it.' While I was sleeping, she put some hair remover gel on my head. I lost handfuls of hair by morning. Patches all over my head! It didn't grow back for months. She never admitted it, but I found the bottle in the wastebasket that morning. She laughed like crazy when my hair fell out. I was so humiliated. Randy cut my hair all over my head so it didn't look so patchy."

"I thought you looked like Twiggy!" Randy teased and then tousled her hair. "It was kinda cute! Ah Sis, this won't be so bad! We can handle it. We have before."

"She has never been this angry before. We're really going to get it. She has put a lot of thought into it. I never did find the necklace that Dad gave me. I know she took it. I remember the look on her face when I asked her if she saw it. I knew she did it."

Randy looked at his sister and said quietly, "I know what she did. She told me one time when I was home on leave."

"Why didn't you tell me?"

"We hadn't talked in a long time. You were married to Dean and there was no communication, remember?" Randy pointed out.

"Yes, I do. Well?"

"Well what?"

"What did she do with it?"

"She put it in the kitty litter box and then asked you to change the box. You threw it out in the trash yourself. She still thinks it's funny," Randy related. "I didn't tell you because I knew it would just upset you all over again."

"I hate her so much! You have no idea! She's a monster, and the nicer she is to you, the more you should watch out! I hope I can tell her off and then never see her again," Diane almost shouted. "Randy, you'll be there with me, won't you?"

"I'll try, Sis. I talked to her counselors and they want to meet with us when we get there. I guess she is causing problems at the facility."

"I'm surprised she hasn't been kicked out of there," Diane stated. "Maybe we should just go and leave Bea and Matt here. They don't need to see her."

"Yes, I do," Bea was adamant. "She's threatened to ruin my life with Randy!"

"I won't sit back and let her destroy you. I've never met her in person, but I've been skewered by her more than once on the phone. I don't want you to do this alone," Matt looked at Diane and then Randy. "Neither one of you. Bea and I are going to make our lives with you, so it is our business."

"You guys are great," Randy said, "But you really have no idea what you're dealing with. None at all."

Bea shook her short brown hair, "I know to never eat anything chocolate and to not go to sleep in her presence. What do you say, Matt? Think we can handle it?"

"Don't know, but I'm willing to try. What time are we leaving tomorrow?"

"When we get up. Oh, I booked us a two-room suite up in Portland. Don't get excited, it's cheap enough so I think it only means that both rooms share the same door!"

"You are so cheap, Berg! That is an adjoining room, not a suite," Matt retorted.

"You call it an adjoining room if you want. I prefer to think of it as a suite."

"Whatever, Flyboy," Matt laughed.

"Besides, what would a priest know about suites?"

"You might just be surprised."

Bea entered the fray, "I'm going to have a talk with my brother Father Bart. I'll get to the bottom of it."

"We better get to bed," Diane suggested. "I'm sorry I started something tonight. I was a beautiful evening until then."

"I am glad you guys finally told us. Don't keep that stuff to yourselves anymore? Have we got your word?" Matt asked.

Everyone nodded and had a four-way handshake.

Stretched out on the futon, Matt asked Randy, "Is your Mom dangerous?"

"Matt, she's evil, and probably insane."

"Oh." Matt answered.

Surprisingly, by six in the morning, the four were heading out of the Big Apple squished inside Randy's blue Crown Deluxe Toyota with all their bags.

"I'm the only one that knows how to pack," Randy boasted. "The Air Force would never allow all these suitcases!"

"They don't look as good as Diane and I do, either," Bea kissed his cheek with a giggle. "Think carefully before you disagree."

"Guess I got told."

Matt chuckled, "I would have warned you, but you sorta deserved it."

"It's nice to know you have my back."

"I'll buy breakfast when we get out of the heavy traffic to make up for it," Matt offered. "Diane and I are both used to eating a big breakfast."

"I remember that from the farm. 'Course you've been up and did chores before then, so it isn't quite the same." Bea remembered.

"Boy, did I love Grandma's caramel rolls," Randy smacked his lips.

"I learned how to make them," Diane's eyes sparkled. "Mine aren't half bad."

"They are almost as good as Grandma's," Matt said.

Diane raised one eyebrow, "Almost? Thank you."

"You're batting a thousand there, Mr. Harrington!" Bea giggled.

"You're still my friend, aren't you?"

"You know, your niece little Miriam calls me 'Be Friend'."

"She did, didn't she?" Diane's face lit up. "Wait until you meet all the new kids! The five-year-old Clarissa thinks everything is the mostest bestest wonderfullest in the whole wide world!"

Matt laughed, "She manages to get it all in almost every sentence! And you haven't lived until you've heard Clancy's wolf howl!"

"You guys," Diane's eyes got huge, "That little guy has woke us up in the middle of the night more than once with his howl. Then the little girls cry! Sleeping at the farmhouse is an experience."

Matt shook his head, "Between Clancy howls, Grandpa's midnight wanderings, the two veterans waking up screaming from war nightmares and now Miss Diane traipsing all over—it is a wonder anyone sleeps."

Diane frowned, "Look Matt, I'm one of the quieter ones. Don't forget, Elton and Clarence are up keeping a lid on everyone else!"

"Who's Clarence?"

"He is the oldest of the Grey Hawk kids. He is eight and a worrywart."

"I remember when I stayed there, Elton was like an old mother hen," Randy nodded. "I had many a cigarette with the man at three in the morning."

"Me too. I mean, I didn't smoke, but he did. He is one of the mostest bestest in the whole, wide world!" Matt grinned and drew swats from everyone in the car. "Alright. I'll be quiet."

The trip north out of New York City was fun. It was reminiscent of a group of college kids heading out for a fun weekend. There was no serious talk and everyone was upbeat. The guys sat in front and the girls curled up in the back. After a big breakfast at a Country Inn, the group became quiet. Within a few miles, the girls were asleep.

Randy looked in the rearview mirror and then asked, "They out?"

Matt nodded, "Snoring and drooling."

"If they'd heard that, your head would be a hood ornament."

Matt stretched, "Yah. Do you think this visit will be bad? I had Diane take a tranquilizer when we stopped for breakfast. Samuels said she has to keep control."

"She does. I don't know what to tell you. You have to keep on your toes around Mom, and you can't trust what you see. Diane's right. The nicer she is; the worse she is. Like when Diane wrote an essay for a scholarship to a summer literature high school program. They were going to hold classes from nine to noon in the summer months. Mom never said that she didn't want her to do it. In fact, she seemed to think it was a good idea. The morning of the deadline, Diane couldn't find her essay. She and I looked all over the place and then I noticed that look on Mom's face. I knew she'd done something. I found the remains of it. She had burned it in the fireplace during the night."

"She's really a piece of work. What did Diane do?"

"Nothing. She never mentioned it again. She didn't want to give Mom the satisfaction."

"Did she have another copy to hand in?"

"No, but I can tell you that neither of us left anything that mattered to us where she could reach it again."

Matt studied Randy's face, "Diane said that you and your Mom had a serious falling out recently. How serious was it?"

"I didn't want to see Mom again. She was so horrible to Bea when we were up here a month ago. Matt, it was beyond—just beyond!" He shook his head, "I went back to see her alone the next time I had off. She was so pleased I was by myself! She really thought that I had dumped Bea. I told her that I was getting married whether she liked it or not. First, she cried those pathetic crocodile tears, which just makes me ill! I told her to knock it off. She instantly became vicious. She told me that she'd see to it that Bea and I never married. I should count on it. I told her to never talk that bad to Bea again. Then she smiled, that 'I just ate your cat' smile and said, 'Oh, you don't have to worry about that.' I told her to sit there alone because she might as well get used to it. I walked out of that place with no intention of seeing her again."

"You're coming back just for Diane?"

"I'd like to say I am, but that's not true. Diane and I are still responsible for her and her bills, etc. Her doctors called me and wanted to meet. Mom has been causing trouble. I have to be here, but Bea came mostly because you guys were coming."

"I think you have a great lady there."

"I'm so damned lucky. I tell you, I don't deserve anyone as good as her. I hope that Diane can see how lucky she is."

"She was good until this trip. I mean, a few spells after talks with your mom, but for the most part, things have been great. She was even beginning to think about our wedding plans and stuff, but since

Loretta got on the phone, there's none of that. She is pulling away big time.

"Why does she still listen to Mom? Most of the time, I try to keep from slamming the receiver in her ear!"

"Because she has it in her head that her mom should love her! She wants that so much."

Randy looked at Matt, "Good grief, I don't think Mom is capable of loving anyone, including herself! It makes me want to shake Di. She should know better."

"Knowledge isn't the issue."

"I know. I really do. Maybe when she sees Mom now that she has something else to compare it to, she'll realize. The only thing Mom wants is someone to cater to her every need, real or imagined and take her constant ridicule. Those folks are few and far between."

"I have to say, I can't imagine this woman. Just the conversations on the phone have driven me to distraction. From my dealings with her, I'm curious how someone so miserable can evoke any sympathy or con anyone."

"I see that. Diane's problem is that still feels guilty about leaving. She really has no reason to feel that way at all. If Mom smells even the hint of guilt, she will zero in and you are doomed. Then since Mr. Waggoner was such a beast, it just confirmed to Diane that she wasn't worthy of human kindness. She would have cracked if it hadn't been for Dr. Samuels."

"That's the truth. Last fall was a nightmare," Matt concurred.

Bea's soft voice entered the conversation as she sat up in the back seat and spoke quietly so Diane wouldn't wake up. "Matt, I hate to say it, but Loretta is an unmitigated bitch, and that is an insult to dogs everywhere. You have to meet her. Randy would have never been able to explain her to me so I could really understand."

"That's one of the reasons that I want to meet her. I think I need to for Diane."

"You guys, she's having an awful time. She tosses, turns and talks in her sleep."

"I know, she has nightmares too," Matt put in.

"Yes," Bea shared. "She's really terrified of what her Mom might do. I think that she is imagining things, but then that woman has surpassed my expectations at every turn. Randy, do you know how bad your Mom was to her after you left for the Air Force?"

"Not much. Diane never wrote anything bad and Mom never said anything good; so their letters weren't revealing. I know from my talks with Dr. Samuels and her last fall, that Mom was worse than she had been when I was still home. I know that Mom broke up every budding relationship Diane ever had with a guy. She'd call and cancel dates or call the guys families and say God knows what. Diane learned by college, not to ever let Mom know if she had a date. She managed to go with Dean without Mom meeting him. Diane was living in the dorm at the university at that time. Mom has never let her forget that she 'sneaked off" to get married."

"I didn't know that. I imagine from what I have learned about the Waggoner family, that Dean didn't really think that was unusual." Matt confided. "From what I heard, he was quiet and withdrawn socially. The only reason that he stayed around Merton was because he worried for his mother's safety. My word, what is with people, anyway? I think that both Diane and Dean wanted a real marriage, but they probably didn't have a chance in hell. Neither had a parent as a role model or a marriage worthy of replication."

"Yah," Randy agreed. "That is why I spent so many years keeping as far away from a commitment as possible. Then old Bea came pirouetting into my life and dang—I was hooked! Of course, I had several rounds of talks with the chaplains in the Air Force and Dr. Samuels. They didn't let me get away with much. Now the Fedder family, they are nice people. They are a lot like the folks in North Dakota. Well you know. You met Bonnie and Beth. Father Bart is one of your best friends. What is it you guys call him?"

Matt laughed, "Slick! He is a real slicker. You guys should have seen him the first time he came out to ride horse! He had new cowboy boots, new blue jeans and a cowboy hat that didn't even have a crease in it! He looked like a real city slicker. And you know Darrell couldn't let that pass! The next day when Bart was giving Mass, he was so saddle sore, he could hardly move! I was killing myself trying to keep from laughing."

They all laughed and then woke Diane. After that, the group talked about everything but Loretta Berg.

It was two-thirty when the little blue Toyota pulled up in front of the Harborview Motel. Matt laughed hysterically, "Yea gads man, you can't even smell the ocean from here! Where's the harbor?"

"Stifle it. You'll be glad when you cough up your half of the nice little bill. It is clean and stuff," Randy stated.

The bill was quite reasonable when the men checked in. They drove the car over by the room, but the girls walked because it felt good to stretch. Randy parked the car and they started taking the bags out. Randy unlocked the room door with a great flourish. Bea was the first to burst out laughing.

There were two stale-smelling rooms side by side. They both opened into a tiny space sided by the bathroom door, closet door and outside door. There was only a small window in one room with a double bed and the larger window in the other over the double bed. The bathroom had a foot square window inside the shower. Each bedroom had a chair and three-drawer, four-foot wide dresser.

The entire place was probably just this side of sanitary and certainly not spotless. There were no doors on the bedrooms as they simply opened into the little space. There wouldn't have been enough room for any more doors to open. The bathroom had a stool, a two-foot square shower and a small sink with a mirror, but no shelves. There were two hand towels and two wash clothes on the rack over the toilet. Matt was carrying the four bath towels the clerk had given him.

Diane cracked up, "Ah, the lap of luxury!"

"It was inexpensive," Matt said trying to keep a straight face.

Randy frowned, "Look, there are pretty flowers out front. So knock it off."

Diane laughed so hard she had tears in her eyes, "You dingbat! Those are dandelions!"

"See if I talk to you guys," Randy blustered.

"What are we going to do now?" Bea asked. "May I make a suggestion?"

Randy scowled and Diane said, "Please do."

"Let's clean up, one at a time, and then grab a burger before we go over to see Mrs. Berg."

"Good idea," Randy agreed sarcastically, "But don't think I didn't catch that 'one-at-a-time' crack!"

Diane giggled, "And be sure not to get your towel too wet because you will have to use it until tomorrow. We do get new ones tomorrow, right?"

Randy grumped, "At any rate, I get to use the bathroom first because I only have one bag, unlike the rest of you!"

He stomped off to the 'guys' bedroom and opened his duffle while the rest howled in laughter. They were getting settled when they heard Randy get into the shower. Then they heard the walls bang when his elbows hit the sides of the little shower. It was only a couple minutes before he yelled a profanity and turned the water off. They heard him in the bathroom mumbling about not enough hot water to get a mosquito wet while they tried to keep their gales of laughter silent.

They all went outside to wait so Randy could have some privacy while he growled around getting dressed. A few minutes later, he opened the door and said, "Okay. You were right. I screwed up. If you want, we can move to another motel."

"No, this is fine," Matt clapped Randy on the shoulder. "It is cheap and close to the care facility."

"There are only about two seconds of hot water. I'm warning you."

Bea gave him a hug, "It's okay, really."

He kissed her cheek, "Don't say I didn't offer."

"We know," Diane smiled. "We need to freshen up a bit and then let's go eat."

"While you gals are doing that, I'm going to walk over the office and ask them if they can fix the hot water."

"Want me to come along?" Matt asked.

"Yah, I guess. We'll let the girls have the place." Randy made a face, "It sounded nice over the phone."

"Don't worry about it." Matt consoled him.

The group walked the four blocks to a hamburger shop. Lunch was much more subdued. They all seemed to be looking ahead, now only a few minutes, to the visit. The care facility was only a couple blocks further down the road.

Everyone had soup and a hamburger except Matt. The soup was a thick clam chowder and Matt was extremely allergic to clams. He contented himself with the hamburger and potato chips. No one had any dessert, deciding to get on their way.

The care facility, Shorepoint, was a huge one-story sprawling brick building. The grounds were manicured beautifully. There were trimmed trees and flowering shrubs with beds of flowers surrounding many patios. The facility sat on top of a bluff with a magnificent view of the ocean. The drop off from the bluff was steep and rocky and the rest of the way to beach was rugged, rocky tidal basin teeming with marine wildlife. It was elegantly picturesque.

"If we have time, I'd like to go walking down there," Matt said as he took Diane's hand. "I love to watch the crabs and all that. Think we can?"

Diane smiled, "Maybe further up the beach, huh? I don't think I'm going to want to be too close to the facility if I can help it."

"Sure," then he looked at his fiancée, "How you doing? Did you take your pill at lunch?"

"Yes I did," Diane nodded. "I don't want to go. I feel like Clarence when the people from Social Services came to check on them and he wanted to run away!"

"I know," Matt squeezed her hand. "If you want to leave at any time or think you can't do it any more, just give me the high sign. The most important thing is for you not to lose control. Got your word?"

She nodded, stopped walking and put her arms around him. She tried to keep from crying into his shoulder, but a few tears sneaked out.

"Hey, you don't want to go in there with big tear-stained eyes! The gig will be up!"

Diane stiffened and took a deep breath. "You're right. I need to remember there is nothing she can do to me. I have you, these guys, and the Engelmann clan and my job and . . ."

"You'll be just fine. Remember that," Matt squeezed her again. "Ready to go on?"

"Yes. No more blubber baby!" she giggled, referring to the expression used by the kids on the farm. "The Grey Hawk kids would say don't be a sooky calf."

Matt smiled, "I've heard them."

The four entered the large foyer and approached the information desk. The room was enormous with several groupings of small sofas. There were two ten-foot long fireplaces on either side. The walls were made of the same brick as the outside and bore huge hooked rugs in dark, earth colors. The desk was to the right of the wide hallway that went all to way to the back patio and the distant view of the ocean.

A neat, friendly lady met them with a smile, "Hello. May I assist you in finding your loved one?"

Randy answered, "Loretta Berg. I know the way, but I need to notify Dr. Werner that my sister and I are here and will be here tomorrow. He said he needed to talk to us. If you could leave him a message, I'd appreciate it. I have our motel room number, too if you want it."

While Randy was giving the information to the lady, Matt was looking around the building. "This place is gorgeous. I've been in and out of a lot of them as a priest and this place really looks good. How is the care?"

Bea nodded, "Excellent. Mrs. Berg should thank her lucky stars. She has no idea what the average human has to deal with."

Matt nodded. Diane had moved to the desk with Randy. "From the phone calls when she complained so much, I would've thought that she was in a dump. I knew Diane and Randy would never tolerate that, but this is spectacular."

The two at the counter joined the others, "We have an appointment with Dr. Werner at ten tomorrow morning. That should be okay, huh?" Randy asked.

"Sounds good to me," Matt smiled.

"Well, let's get this behind us," Randy announced. "Bea, if Mom is so mean to you again, you have my permission to slap her."

"Oh Randy, I wouldn't do that. She can't help being a bitch. I am just glad I'm not like her."

They walked a long way after turning off the main hall. They must have walked half a mile down another long hallway before they got to her room. On the door was a nameplate that said, "Loretta Berg, Room 1145."

"How many residents does the place have?" Matt asked.

"When she first arrived, there were five hundred," Randy explained, "But now they have over a thousand. It is nice because when they build a new wing, the older residents get first pick of the new rooms. Almost all the rooms have a spectacular view."

They took a collective sigh and Randy knocked before he opened the oak door.

# 4

Randy entered the room first, with Diane following. Then Matt followed Bea. Inside the room, Randy said, "Hello Mom. Look who I have with me!"

The small lady in the wheelchair was looking out the window. Slowly she turned her electric wheelchair around toward them. Matt tried not to stare.

The skinny woman was a little shorter than Diane, about five-three, but couldn't have weighed ninety pounds. She had fine, severe features. Her dyed blue-black hair was a stark contrast to her extremely pale skin. Even with too much make-up, it was almost a translucent white and the blue veins showed through. The skin over her face was taut and seemed stretched to the point of breaking. Her eyebrows were as dark as her hair, over squinty ghostly pale gray eyes, ringed with thick black eyeliner. Her lipstick was a bright scarlet red.

She wore a black crepe dress with a white lace Peter Pan collar and cuffs on the three quarter length sleeves. The dress was the style of a young schoolgirl with a tightly pleated bodice and a softer pleated knee-length skirt. Her legs couldn't have been any bigger around than Matt's wrist. She wore white hose that didn't conceal the age spots and varicose veins on her bony legs. She wore black shiny patent leather shoes that anyone could see weren't used for walking.

Her arms from her elbows to her age-spotted hands were extremely wrinkled and porcelain colored. The blood vessels ran back and forth across the back of her hands in a blue network. Her nails were very long and painted with a bright scarlet polish. Instead of looking classy, it gave her already grotesque appearance a creepy quality.

Randy approached his Mom and bent down to kiss her cheek. She said nothing. He asked her, "How do you like your new electric wheelchair?"

"It's adequate," she said weakly.

Then Diane approached, "Hello Mom."

Mrs. Berg barely lifted her head to see her daughter, and almost wimpered, "Nice of you to find time to see me."

Diane bent down to hug her and Mrs. Berg pulled back. She reprimanded her daughter with great strength in her voice, "Your breath is atrocious! You need a breath mint!"

Diane moved back and Mrs. Berg moved her eyes toward the door. She glared at Bea, but only spoke to Randy, "You simply don't learn, do you?"

Bea was undaunted and started to cross the fifteen-foot room. Mrs. Berg turned the chair and pushed the button. She drove the chair rapidly toward her and didn't stop until she had cracked the protruding metal footrests into Bea's shins. Bea jumped back, "You need to practice driving that chair!"

Mrs. Berg gave her a determined look, "You're rather ungainly for a dancer."

Matt was flabbergasted but turned his attention to the woman who had noticed him and was approaching. He wondered if he should hide his legs behind a chair, but she stopped within a respectable distance. Apparently, she somehow gained more control over her chair. She almost sneered, "So this is the heretic priest my daughter goes on about! Doesn't look like much to me!"

Matt mustered a smile and held out his hand, "It is nice to put a face to the voice on a phone, Mrs. Berg."

She looked at his hand with disdain, "You could care less! Don't lie! However, I don't suppose that's any worse than breaking all your other vows. I'm curious, which did you prefer: nuns or pubescent boys?"

Matt withdrew his hand and tried to keep from making a fist. He knew she was baiting him and he didn't want to give in. There was no question in his mind that he certainly didn't like her. Bea was right; she was an unmitigated bitch.

Randy was checking out Bea's shins. They were both swelling rapidly and the skin was broken on each leg where footrests smashed into them. "Need some ice for them?" Randy asked.

"Oh quit fussing!" Mrs. Berg ordered. "She's a big girl. As clumsy as she is, I'm sure she deals with bruises all the time. You sure took your time getting here. Judging from Diane's foul breath, you all just ate. Nice of you to think of me."

"We hadn't eaten since morning. We'll take you out for dinner later," Randy suggested. "Does that sound good?"

"What did you eat without me?"

Diane answered, "We stopped at a hamburger place. Everyone except Matt had soup and sandwich."

Mrs. Berg scowled at Matt, "Are you too good for that?"

"No, I'm extremely allergic to clams and all they had is clam chowder. So I just had a hamburger."

The frail woman got a peculiar look on her face and then smiled smugly. She turned her chair to her son, "I'd like to go out tonight with you all. The Clam Shell is a nice restaurant from what I hear. They serve all sorts of shellfish."

"Mom!" Diane started.

Mrs. Berg snapped, "Don't you start with me, you selfish, sniveling whore."

Matt stepped forward, "That sort of talk isn't appropriate."

"You have no say in how I speak to my negligent daughter. Have you ever fathered anything? You don't know a thing."

Randy stood up, "Okay Mom. We're leaving. You can just sit here alone. I don't personally give a damn. You deliberately drove into Bea. We all know that. I should've never bothered with you."

"I'm not the one in need of regaining good graces. It's your irrational sister. She has never been capable of maintaining her composure more than a week in her entire life."

Randy helped Bea to her feet and headed toward the door. Matt held out his hand to Diane and they started to leave. Just before they went through the open door, Mrs. Berg called out. "Okay, okay! I overreacted! I was simply embarrassed that I accidentally hit Beatrice's legs. I didn't know what to do. May we start over?"

Randy wanted to leave, but Bea and Diane both thought they should stay. He reluctantly came back in and walked right up to his mother in threatening manner, "You do one thing out of line and we leave forever. I mean it."

She started to cry and he just rolled his eyes. "You know how much I hate that bullshit. Just stop!"

Bea tried to calm everyone, "Okay, let's try again."

The four young people sat down in the living area on the overstuffed love seat and chairs. Diane tried to make conversation, "This is a nice room. You have a wonderful view. How long have you been in this room?"

"Over a year. It isn't as nice as it looks. Everything is cheap and the cleaning service is inept. These large patio windows only get cleaned once a week. Most of the time, you can't see out of them," Mrs. Berg complained. "The staff must all live in squalor themselves because they don't care about anything."

Randy changed the subject, "When did you get your new wheelchair?"

"Three days ago. I only got it because the staff didn't like having to push me. You know, I'm too weak to handle the other chair. I prayed daily that my children would come and take me into their lives, instead of leaving me alone with uncaring strangers."

"There is a retirement home in Merton, but it isn't nearly as nice as this place," Matt suggested.

"I don't deserve to live in an institution. I gave up my life for my children. They should take care of me in their home. Why on earth would I want to be in a cattle shed in the middle of the prairies? That isn't my home."

"Mom, as soon as I'm out of the service, I'm moving out to the prairies. Diane already lives there. If you want to be near us, you need to be there, too," Randy explained.

"My home is here. You cannot abandon me like you did before! I've forgiven you of that, but you need to look to my needs now." Mrs. Berg continued. "You could get a large enough home so I could live with my own children."

"Mom, we aren't children anymore. We are adults and need to have our own lives," Diane responded.

Matt was so proud of her, but Mrs. Berg was livid. "You impudent sow! You don't know the first thing about it! You owe it to me. Look what you got for defying me before! It is no wonder that those people had to discipline you. You're lucky you only got thrown down the stairs!"

"Mom, you have no right to say that! I didn't deserve what Waggoner did; or for that matter, how you treated me! This is enough of this. We all bit out tongues and came to see you even though you are a miserable human being. You don't seem to understand that *you* need to be good to us. I won't be cowed by you any longer. Matt, let's leave." Diane stood up and her mom's jaw dropped.

This time, they all walked out of the room and down the hall. Bea was limping and Diane was fighting back her tears, but they felt good about their decision.

Once in the hallway, Randy said, "Would you like me to go get the car, Bea? Your legs are really swollen."

"No, actually walking would feel good. When we get to the room, I'll ice them down. I have to keep them moving though. I have to dance on Wednesday night." After a few steps, Bea said, "I shouldn't have come in today. I know she hates me."

"It was no way your fault! She was awful," Randy said. "No one should ever visit that wizened old shrew."

Diane had quit crying and then said, "I think I stood up to her, huh?"

Matt gave her a hug, "Yes, you did. I was proud of you. Do you think you'll never see her again?"

Randy groaned, "I only wish. No, we have to see her in the morning. I need to stop by the desk and tell them we're going now. The old bag will probably work herself into a state or something."

At the desk, Randy stopped and explained to the lady what happened, minus the insults. The woman didn't seem surprised and nodded. "Will you be at your motel if we need to speak to you?"

"Yes, we're going there now."

As they turned to leave, the lady noticed Bea's limp. "Ma'am, please have a seat. I'd like to have a nurse check your legs."

"They're fine," Bea said.

"No, they aren't. Please have a seat. She ran into with her wheelchair, didn't she?"

They all nodded the affirmative. The lady took a deep breath, "It happens more than we care to say. It'd be best if we checked it out. Liability and all. We have a nurse and doctor on staff."

Randy nodded, "You should, Bea."

Matt agreed and then said, "Hey, why don't Diane and I go get the car and bring it back? By then, you should be all checked out."

Bea rubbed her shins, "I feel like a wimp."

Diane giggled, "That's my job, remember? We'll be right back."

"Thanks," Randy said as he handed Matt the keys.

Out in the brisk, sunny day, Matt and Diane started walking back to their motel. It was a couple blocks before either said anything. Then Matt said, "That was an experience. I think that she aimed for Bea. What do you think?"

Diane nodded. After a few minutes she said, "She knows that dancing is important to Bea. If she is bruised badly enough, she won't be able to dance. Typical Mom."

"Really? Diane, did she do that kind of stuff a lot?"

"I don't know what you mean by a lot. If we had any interests or anything that took out attention from her, she would exact requitement. If we were smart enough, we tried not to let her know that we cared about anything but her. Then we were okay."

Matt shook his head, "Unbelievable."

"Waggoners weren't as subtle. Wag just belted you when something made him mad, but he didn't connive. Mom can put a lot of time into getting her revenge."

"No wonder you are afraid of her."

"I really never imagined that she'd try to hurt Bea. I mean, I knew she'd try to break them up," then Diane gave Matt a hug. "I'm so sorry she talked that way to you."

"I wasn't surprised. She's said pretty much the same on the phone from time to time. You know, sticks and stones—No one would ever imagine by looking at her that she is such a serpent. She doesn't look soft and fuzzy, but she looks too weak to do what she does."

Diane blurted out, "She is one hell of a lot stronger than you think. I wish Dr. Samuels could meet her."

"That would be interesting. Did you notice that in her room, she had not one photo or item that's in any way personal?" Matt asked.

"Nothing. She has a nice place. That living area is as big as our cabin. I almost chuckled when she was talking about getting a big enough house for you all to live in! Can you imagine her in our cabin?"

Diane laughed, "She wouldn't be caught dead in there!"

They got to the motel, picked up the car and were back to the Shorepoint Care Center in about twenty-five minutes. When they came into the lobby, the receptionist directed them to Consult Room 631. One of the doctors wanted to meet them there.

Diane and Matt went down the hall and found the room. They knocked and then Matt opened the door slightly.

"Come in," Dr. Werner called. "Diane and Matt, is it?"

"Yes," they said as they came in.

Dr. Werner stood at the large conference table, motioned for them to take a seat and shook their hands. "I just spoke with Randy. He and Bea will be here momentarily. I came back from seeing Mrs. Berg and would like to talk to you all. So you are out here from South Dakota?"

"North Dakota," Matt corrected. "We are both from the East originally, however."

"Maine?"

"I'm from Maine, but Matt is a Massachusetts boy," Diane smiled. "We both live in central North Dakota now, and love it."

"I have a friend who was born and raised in North Dakota. Where was it? Grand something, over the border from Canada."

"Grand Forks?"

"Yes, that's it. Is that near where you live?"

"About two hundred miles, on the northeast side of the side," Matt answered as there was another knock on the door.

Bea and Randy entered and found seats. Both Bea's legs were taped. She seemed to be walking better.

Matt looked at her, "How are the legs?"

Bea shrugged but Randy answered, "Bruised real good. The doctor said she can't dance until Thursday at the earliest. He called the theatre."

"I think I could," Bea said.

"No, the doctor said the right shin might even be cracked. You need to take it easy," Randy frowned.

"I'm sorry that you were injured." Dr. Werner said, "I hope that you'll recover soon, but I think that you should follow the doctor's advice."

"Yes, I will, but I still think I could do it."

Dr. Werner cleared his throat, "I feel like I'm representing the wrong side here, because I do understand how you must all be feeling. Apparently, your short visit with Mrs. Berg was very contentious."

Randy's face hardened, "You could describe it that way. I have another word for it."

"I understand." The counselor continued, "I was called to your mother's room a few minutes after you left. She was hysterical and having difficulty breathing. It took a bit, but I finally got her calmed down enough to talk to her. This is what I found. She said she had looked forward to the visit for a couple weeks and was very excited to see everyone. She had arranged to have her hair and nails done and put a great effort into getting dressed for the occasion. It was all she thought about for a while. She was looking forward to it with her whole being and then when she accidentally smashed into Bea's legs, she freaked out. She knows how important Bea's legs are to her career. She admitted that she lost it and started saying unkind things."

"She was saying unkind things before she ran purposely into Bea," Randy stated emphatically. "She may have been looking forward to seeing us, but she unleashed a barrage of insults from the time we walked in the door."

Werner nodded, "She does do that. I've been on the receiving end a time or two. She can be extremely unpleasant. I don't know if she intended to run into Bea. She has run into several people and things since she got her new chair. So, could you give her the benefit of the doubt? She said that you had planned to go out to dinner before she ran into Bea."

"It was afterwards, but she got all rude again." Diane said, "I was the one that wanted to leave then."

"She is afraid that she may never see you again. She couldn't take that. You are all she has. Would it be possible to take her to dinner tonight? I extracted a promise from her that she would mind her tongue. I know it will take a lot on your part, but she couldn't bear to know she would never see you again. She fights depression all the time. I have given her something and she is napping now. I'm certain that when she wakes up, she will be in a better mood if you will give her a chance."

The four looked back and forth at each other, mumbling to each other, "It is up to you."

No one would say yes, and finally Dr. Werner stepped in. "Okay. I will tell her that you're not taking her to dinner. She can eat here. May I tell her that you will see her again? Never is a long time. She seems to be truly repentant and distraught about this."

Randy wagged his head, "We have to see her tomorrow at that meeting with her doctors anyway."

"What about dinner tonight?"

"Let's say yes," Diane said. "But with some ground rules. She cannot take her electric chair. Is there a regular chair we can use? If she starts in about anything, we'll bring her right back here. I know you have no idea, but that woman is much more destructive than you can imagine."

Randy was adamant, "She can have whatever kind of breakdown she wants then."

"Okay. I'll tell her. Thanks, I know she can be difficult. I hope it goes well. If she seems to be argumentative, I'll let you know. Are you going back to your motel now?"

"Yes."

"Okay, I'll call you there after I talk to her. Is that acceptable? I will find a wheelchair and leave it at the front desk for you."

No one spoke all the way back to the motel. Randy asked Matt to go for a walk with him. They walked a short ways before Randy threw a fit. "That miserable old bag suckered the doctor into this! Matt, one of these days, I am gonna wring her neck!"

Matt patted his shoulder, "I understand completely. Regardless, let's just get through this and not let her ruin our time together. Will Bea be okay?"

"She was heartbroken about missing the performance, but she'll survive. She has things in perspective. She said some things are more important than getting a better role as a dancer, but she shouldn't have to! She never did one thing wrong. Hell, she was nicer to Mom than I was! She was a total victim."

"I know. Maybe if we keep her out of your mother's reach and keep your mom out of that electric wheelchair, we can tolerate her flurry of insults. Is Bea resting now?"

"Yah, she was going to take a nap. I said I'd call a restaurant, but we aren't going to the Clam Shell. That was one of her nasty slams. Think we should go ask the desk clerk?"

"Good idea. Randy, are you okay?"

"I don't even know anymore. I get so fed up with the woman. It is horrible to say, but sometimes when the phone rings, I hope it is the call that she has passed away."

"How old is she?"

"Hell, she's only fifty nine. She will see us all to our graves!"

Matt chuckled sardonically, "She'll probably *put* us in our graves!"

The young men returned to their rooms and the girls were getting settled for a nap. "Do you feel better now?" Bea asked as she gave Randy a kiss on the cheek.

"Yes, I erupted to Matt, so now he has to deal with it. How do you feel?"

"I took that pain pill at the Shorepoint and am feeling a little groggy now. Did you make the reservation?"

"Yes, we reserved a place called the Angus Room. The room clerk said it is a good place and has wheelchair access," Randy answered.

Diane said, "Oh, Werner called. He got the wheelchair and said that Mom was extremely grateful that we'd give her another chance. He said he really came down hard on her. He thinks she realizes how close she came to devastating her relationship with her children completely. He told us however, not to bend. If she starts to be vindictive, we should leave as threatened. Or better yet, just take her home and then let her know that everyone else was going to finish their dinner without her."

"I can live with that," Randy said. "I'm glad that it isn't too far away from Shorepoint. We can probably deliver her back there before we get to our salads!"

Matt shook his head, "Being optimistic?"

Randy helped Bea get her foot up on the pillow so she could take a rest, and Matt and Diane went for walk. They found a wooden seat and sat down. Diane cuddled under his arm.

"Do you think I would've had the courage to tell Mom without the tranquilizer?"

Matt chuckled, "You sure told Bart where the gravel met the asphalt that night!"

"I did, huh?" Diane giggled. "He ended up being one of our best friends."

Matt leaned down and kissed her neck and soon they were necking. "Diane, I never realized how malicious your mother was."

"I know. Hey, what time is the reservation?"

"Seven-thirty. Why?"

"We should go back to the room to get ready. I should take another one of my pills? It will take a while for us all to get ready. Is this a dressy place?"

"Sounds like it." Matt stood up, "Okay, let's go back."

# 5

It was quarter past seven when the men brought Mrs. Berg to the car. Randy lifted his tiny mother from the chair into the front seat, while Matt put the chair in the trunk and got in the back seat.

"Where are the women?" Mrs. Berg asked. She was being very polite and respectful.

"They decided to meet us there to give you more room in the car," Randy answered.

"That was thoughtful," the woman acknowledged.

It was only a four-block drive to the restaurant and when they pulled up to the front, she said, "I thought we were going to the Clam Shell."

"We asked at the motel and they said this place is much better. You can still order seafood here." Randy explained as he lifted her back into the chair.

Matt pushed her inside the entrance while Randy parked the car. The host said he had just seated the girls and would show them to the table.

The place was very nice. It had oiled walnut paneling and plush carpet. The tables had long, white tablecloths and fine china. There were Waterford Lighting Coils on each table. It was beautiful.

The waiter removed the chair next to Matt for Mrs. Berg's chair. The waiter brought their menus, iced water, fresh-baked rolls and butter. The conversation was pleasant and Bea was seated as far away from Mrs. Berg as possible. Randy sat next to his fiancée and held her hand while they looked at the menu. Matt sat between Diane and Mrs. Berg.

Mrs. Berg made it a point to be as pleasant as possible. She asked about Bea's family and then Matt's. She expressed an interest in their lives. Matt could see that Randy and Diane were both relieved and in a few minutes seemed to be enjoying the evening.

After they gave their orders, the waiter explained there was a marvelous salad bar. They were welcome to go fill their plates whenever they were ready.

Diane asked her mother what she wanted and she said, "I don't know what they are offering, dear."

Matt looked at the offerings and then returned to tell her. She chose a few items and Diane said she'd go get them for her. Mrs. Berg watched as Randy, Bea and Diane left to fill their salad plates. Matt started to get up and Mrs. Berg asked sweetly if he would mind waiting with her, so she didn't have to sit alone.

He smiled, "No problem. I can get my salad later."

She put her hand on his leg and patted it, "You are a kind young man. So what do you do since you left the church?"

"I teach at the same high school where Diane teaches."

"That's nice," she said, and he was shocked to feel her hand move up toward his groin.

He frowned and moved his leg. She was not dissuaded and put her hand directly in his crotch and began to massage it. He reached under the table and grabbed her hand, "Excuse me."

The gnarly, bony woman purred, "I thought you might want a real woman; someone who has had a lot of experience."

Matt moved her hand to her lap, "What the hell are you doing?"

"We can be very close, if you'd like," she said coyly as her hand moved seductively back to his crotch.

He grabbed it roughly to remove it, "Keep your hand to yourself or I'll break it without remorse," he said through clenched teeth with a smile.

Her expression was unimaginably innocent, which made him detest her even more. He continued to talk to her through his clenched smile, "You know what you were told. We'll take you home."

She laughed, "No you won't. You'd never say anything in front of Diane and Bea. I know better. You're ridiculous."

"Do it again and see," he warned.

It was either what he said or the fact that the girls were coming back to the table; but she put both hands on the table. Matt got up and left for the salad bar immediately.

When he returned, he scooted his chair as close as possible beside Diane and then moved his legs toward her. He was just short of turning his back on Loretta. The girls didn't notice, but Randy gave him an odd look. Matt didn't make eye contact with Randy.

About halfway through dinner, he began to relax. All the while, Loretta was friendly and almost fun. She was chatting away to the girls, attentive and sweet as possible.

When the waiter came to clear some plates away, Matt readjusted his position to normal. As soon as the waiter moved behind Bea and Randy, Loretta shifted her hand into Matt's crotch again. This time she was not seductive, but clenched into his privates with the strength of Hercules. She drilled her nails in as far as she could and twisted. Matt nearly passed out, but he grabbed her hand and swore, "Dammit to hell!"

He rushed to the restroom as fast as he could. He was splashing cold water on his face when Randy came in. "You sick, Matt? You look like you got your balls caught in a revolving door."

Matt leaned back against the wall, "I did."

"What the hell happened?"

"Your mom. I don't know how to say this. When you guys went to get the salad, she fondled me and made a blatant pass. I moved her away. Just now, she grabbed me and dug her claws into me as hard as she could. Don't let anyone tell you she's weak!"

Randy turned his back and froze. Matt looked at him, "I'm so sorry. I shouldn't have said anything. I mean she is your mother. I don't—"

"Matt, I know. She used to do it to me," Randy said somberly as he turned to face Matt. "That's why I left for the service. I was afraid to be near her."

"Did you tell anyone?"

"Hell no," Randy said in exasperation. "Who would I tell? Diane? Not bloody likely! What should we do?"

"I need a minute. I tell you, I almost passed out."

"I'm going out there and take her home. You take your time until you feel a bit better."

"What are you going to say?"

"Don't know," Randy was definite. "Mom knows what she did and the girls are both adults. You take a minute. Okay?"

Matt came out after a few minutes. Mrs. Berg and Randy were gone, but the girls were having coffee. Bea held out her hand to Matt kindly, "Randy told me and after they left, I told Diane. Guess she doesn't like either one of us."

"Guess not. I'm sorry."

"What are you sorry for? She did it, not you." Diane said, "I feel so embarrassed. Are you okay?"

"A little tender, but okay. I could really use a cup of that coffee."

Diane poured him some coffee. Matt took a sip and then asked, "Did Randy say anything to her?"

"No. He whispered to me what happened and then simply went over, took Loretta's fork out of her hand, moved her chair back and wheeled her out of here," Bea explained. "I think she was shocked."

"I know I was," Diane said. "Mom never said a word."

They had finished their coffee by the time Randy came back. "I need a drink. Anyone join me?"

"I can't because of my pain pills," Bea said.

"Me either, because of my pills," Diane added, "I think that Matt is more than ready for a couple straight shots!"

"That I am." Matt looked at Randy, "Was there a scene?"

"No. I never said a word to her. She started to cry and I just kept going. I took her to the desk and asked they see her back to her room. The girl was calling for an attendant as I left. I never said goodbye or anything. Neither did she. With your permission Matt, I'm telling Dr. Werner tomorrow," Randy said.

"No. I will. We need to tell him the foul things that she says, too." Matt pointed out. "We can't expect them to understand if we don't give them the entire picture."

When they got back to the motel, Randy said, "This old dump looks pretty darned good tonight. I've had it. Tomorrow morning, the meeting and then I'm all done with her."

"Can we set it up so we don't have to deal with her ourselves anymore?" Diane asked hopefully.

"I think we can."

"Let's do it then."

The night was long and painful for both Matt and Bea. She was up with her swollen shins several times. Matt was swelling also, but by about four in the morning, was beginning to feel better. Randy woke up and looked over at his friend. "I was worried I might have to take you to the emergency room during the night."

Matt snorted, "That would be a trip I'd really not want to take! Can you imagine explaining to some burly orderly how the injury occurred? No way in hell would I want to say the perpetrator was a tiny invalid!"

Randy started to laugh and could hardly contain himself. "I can't wait for you to tell Elton! I want to be there! Or Darrell!"

"Yah, I don't want to even tell Ian. Yea gads, I'll never hear the end of it! I might just swear everyone to secrecy! I fully understand why you never told anyone. At first, she acted like maybe she wanted to have an affair with me, or something."

"She was probably hoping for that. Can you imagine how horrible that would be for Diane? That would definitely break you two up and hurt Diane at the same time. Sounds like a perfect scenario for Mom."

"What did she want from you?" Matt asked seriously.

"Maybe she thought that I'd never leave her," Randy spoke without emotion. "She could control me. I don't know and I don't want to know. I couldn't wait to get out of there. Honestly, that's why I left the way I did. I know it wasn't fair to Di, but I didn't know what to do. If I had told anyone, Mom would've denied it. She is the manipulator extraordinaire! I have to say, it never once went through my head what she would do to Di."

"I'm sure making passes at any guy who was interested in her would be damaging enough. I wonder if that's why Diane never introduced Dean to her?"

"Probably," Randy shrugged. "I just hope you didn't sustain any major damage. Bea's right shin is massively swollen. If it's okay with you, I thought I'd take her to the emergency room. It doesn't look very good. It is still only four-thirty, so you should try to get some sleep."

"What time do we have to be at the Shorepoint for that meeting?"

"Ten. Dr. Werner said that he was ordering breakfast for us from a local sandwich place that specializes in that. We won't last that long, so I'll grab a snack after I take Bea in. Okay?"

"Ask Diane. I do think I need to sleep some more." Matt started to turn over into his pillow, "Randy, you're a good guy. I'll be proud to have you for a brother-in-law."

Randy chuckled and lobbed a tee shirt at him, "Back at you."

Matt was drifting off when he heard Randy and Bea leave and then heard Diane go into the bathroom. A couple minutes later, he felt Diane's hand on his shoulder. "Honey, I'm going across to the office to the vending machine. I need some coffee. Want something?"

Matt pulled her down to him and he gave her a passionate kiss. She returned his kiss and then he groaned in pain.

Diane sat up, "Okay Casanova, what about your injury? Should you really be doing this?"

"No. I shouldn't. I love you so much." Matt shook his head, "Coffee would be great. Need me to come along?"

"I got it. I'll be right back," She kissed his cheek.

She returned a few minutes later and Matt was in the shower. When he came out, she had his coffee and a very stale roll waiting for him. He picked it up, "Dual purpose?"

She frowned, "What are you talking about?"

"This can be eaten or used for paving streets." He tore the paper off. "Can it be eaten?"

"I devoured mine," Diane giggled, "I may have chipped a tooth, so be careful."

They sat on the edge of the bed and had their breakfast in silence. Brushing the crumbs off the bedspread, Matt asked, "How bad is Bea's shin? Randy seemed very concerned."

"It was even more swollen and where the skin is broken, it was beginning to fester. She told me the doctor at the Shorepoint Care Center was worried that shin bone, what is it? The tibia?"

Matt nodded affirmative.

"The tibia may have received a hairline splinter fracture. If that's the case, she might not be able to dance for a few months."

"Oh Diane," Matt's face fell. "That's horrible. How about the other leg?"

"It wasn't as bad; simply bruised. They'll have to X ray today and find out for sure."

"I doubt I'll ever view little fragile people in wheelchairs the same again," he shook his head. "Want to go for a walk or make out?"

"You're such a jerk!" Diane laughed. "I'm going to pick up in the bathroom and then maybe we can go for a walk. Maybe we can watch the sunrise from that wooden bench on the point."

They were just returning from a short walk, when the little blue Toyota turned in to the parking lot. They walked over to the car and saw Randy helping Bea with her crutches. She got out of the car sporting a lightweight cast on her right leg. Diane ran over to the car, "Oh no! It was cracked?"

"Yes, and I'm blessed with this doggone cast for about six weeks and crutches for three months." Bea grumped and then her face lit up, "The good news is—now I have weapons! Maybe I can defend myself with these crutches."

Matt kissed her cheek, "I'm so sorry. I can't imagine how you feel."

"I called the theatre. I'm on medical leave until next week. Then I need to check in with their doctor and he'll set me up with some exercises I can do without my right leg. I need to keep as fit as possible."

Randy came around the car and put his arm around her waist, "My girl is a trooper. If I was her, I don't know if I'd be as nice about it as she is."

"Wait 'til the pills wear off," Bea giggled. "Besides, getting mad won't change the condition of my leg. I just want it to heal correctly so I can dance again. Hey, can I borrow a lawn mower?"

"Huh?"

"A riding one! I can chase your mom around the Care Center! We could have a demolition derby!"

They all laughed and helped Bea into their room, but no one thought it was very funny.

"What are we going to eat? I'm starving to death! Supper got all messed up last night," Randy complained. "I'll never last another four hours. Shall we just go to that diner and get a little breakfast?"

"I'm game," Diane said. "We have no idea how big those sandwiches will be or anything."

"I know I need something to eat. I have so many pills in me right now, I clink when I walk," Bea pointed out.

The four were all rather quiet over breakfast. They were tired or in pain. Matt was amazed that one tiny person the size of a gnat had decimated four young, fit people in less than twenty-four hours.

After breakfast, they headed back to the room for a short nap and then to get ready to go to the meeting.

# 6

Loretta woke early and lay staring out the large, sliding glass door. It was a pretty morning. Spring was nice and the bulbs would be blooming soon. She liked spring. It made her feel that everything was possible and she had massive plans for the summer.

The last couple days hadn't worked as she wanted. She had hoped Randy would've gotten over that silliness with that skinny broad. She figured she must be good in bed, because she sure wasn't much to look at. And her build! Loretta sniffed, "Her legs look like a skinned bullfrog! Can't be anything attractive about that! Randy always was an imbecile. He's a good-looking man with a fine build, but a total dullard. Too much like his worthless father."

She rolled over in bed and debated about whether she should get up on her own, or call for help. She didn't feel like working very hard, but she had a lot of things to get done and didn't want an audience. No, she wouldn't call for help.

She sat up and pulled the pillows under her head. She was surprised that Matt was nice looking. She didn't think Diane had it in her to attract anything that hadn't slithered out of skid row. Must be something wrong with him. He was kicked out of the Catholic church! She laughed quietly, "I can see him banging a little boy. What is that stupid daughter of mine thinking? She couldn't keep a real man. So, maybe she thinks she has a chance with this miscreant."

Loretta detested him. She hadn't like him when they talked on the phone. He was always so protective of Diane and Randy for that matter. What was it to him? Those kids had a God-given responsibility to her and they needed to live up to it.

"They aren't much, but the bloodsucking leeches owe it to me to take care of me. They should buy a house and both work. One should work nights, so they could care for me round the clock. They seem to think they're special and that's why I want them around. Hell, I'd be better off if I could get my money out of their control, buy my own place and hire that Guinea kid Antonio that works here. Now he could take care of me, and maybe even make it fun."

She sat up and continued mumbling to herself, "Too bad I can't. I really screwed up there. I didn't realize that I was signing control of that money over to them when I asked them to take responsibility of my affairs. I should've hired a better lawyer."

She pulled herself out of bed and weakly moved over to the wheelchair. "Those little bastards saw to it that I don't have my good wheelchair anymore! I should've hit that muscle-bound twinkle-toes harder the first time. Didn't have a good enough run for it. Oh well, I think she got the point. It will be awhile before she can dance on her toes!"

She wheeled over to a small desk and retrieved her phone book. She looked up the local grocery store that made deliveries to the patients at the Shorepoint Care Center. The residents all had small refrigerators and a hot plate in their room, so they could make snacks for themselves. They also ordered toiletries, cosmetics, magazines and books. The store charged a delivery fee and one was expected to leave a tip for the pimply-faced teenager who delivered. Today, it would be worth every penny.

Loretta got the man on the phone and gave her order, "I'd like the following items, delivered immediately. I'm having guests unexpectedly and realize that I need these things now."

"Okay Ma'am. We can get it there within the hour."

"Make sure. I want couple nice lemons, nothing shriveled like the last time I ordered. A six-pack of that canned tomato juice, some celery stalks, a small bottle of Tabasco sauce and a four-ounce bottle of pure clam juice. That is pretty tasteless by itself, right?"

"The clam juice? I don't know, it tastes like clams, but it is not an overpowering taste."

"It is pure, right? Not some knock off?"

"Yes Ma'am. Totally pure. It will be good in Bloody Marys."

Loretta smiled and nodded, "Okay. Also, one of those atomized bottles of that perfume Argpege by Lanvin. Could I get a pint of

Vodka? I sure wish this joint would let us order more than a pint at a time! Anyway, large bag of potato chips and container of garlic sour cream dip."

"Okay Ma'am. It'll be there as soon as possible."

After exchanging the necessary information, Loretta hung up and put the phone book away. Then she got out her wallet and counted out the money. With great relish, she set two crisp dollar bills out for the delivery boy.

"It will be a great celebration today when I finally get rid of these irritating impediments. By sunset, my kids will be turning to me for comfort and forgiveness. They are so malleable; it was almost a boring contest. I have to say, Matt is more of a challenge. It might have been interesting to have him live with us. Well, he'll soon know he shouldn't have spurned my offer. Now he has to face his requitement."

She knew he was a threat, so he needed to disappear. If Randy realized that she wasn't toying with him, she could likely get him to dump Bea for Bea's sake. And Diane. That little skank needed to pay for walking out on her! She needed a big loss that would make a big impression. Something to remember! She was certain she had been too accommodating to her children and now that would all change. Starting today! Loretta had just the thing in mind.

Loretta got dressed with great care. She wanted to wear the perfect thing for her great moment. She chose a scarlet red pantsuit with a white, silky blouse. She brushed her hair and applied her makeup. Today, she fixed her eye makeup with bold black liner, blue eye shadow and stark black mascara. As she put her lashes in the curler, she said, "Too bad that Diane, the worthless tramp, got the long eyelashes. She is such a Pollyanna! She doesn't have any idea how to use her feminine charms. She's about as enticing as a harbor seal."

She opened the door when the delivery boy knocked and snapped, "Did you check to make sure it is all there?"

"I did."

Mrs. Berg scowled at him, "Do it again in front of me so I know that you didn't cheat me!"

The teen patiently went through all her items and she nodded. "Good. Now, please open the bottles. Sometimes I cannot get them open."

"Which ones?"

"The Tabasco, clam juice and vodka, you dolt."

The lad did and asked her if it was okay.

She nodded and handed him the tip, "Here's something for your trouble. Now get your bony ass out of here."

The kid smiled and went to the door, "Be happy to."

She slammed the door and wondered if she should call his boss and complain about his insolence, but decided against it. She had too many things to do. She put the groceries away except the clam juice. She rechecked the screw cap and then securely closed it. She wrapped the bottle in a scarf and tucked it in the seat of her wheel chair.

She smothered herself in the perfume and called the front desk.

"This is Loretta Berg. I was wondering which consulting room we'd be meeting in this morning."

"We'll be sending someone to get you when it is time, Mrs. Berg."

"I want to go there myself. You people always harangue me because I don't move around enough! You are impossible to please. Now I want to go on my own. Tell me where it is!"

"I'll find it for you. Could you hold please?"

Loretta drummed her long fingernails on the tabletop and waited impatiently. When the girl came back on the phone, Loretta snapped, "Did you have to have someone explain the English language to you?"

"No Ma'am," the girl said patiently. "I just wanted to check to make certain I gave you the correct information. Your meeting will be in Consult Room 45 at ten o'clock."

"They are ordering breakfast, right? From Sunrise Sandwiches?"

"Yes. I just called and got the orders from your children. I was about to call you when you rang. Which would you like?"

"What are the others having?"

The girl sighed and read off the list, "Let's see. Randy is having the Denver Omelet sandwich, Bea is having a Club Breakfast, Diane is having a Sausage and Buttermilk Biscuit and Matt is having Eggs Benedict."

Loretta said, "That last one sounds interesting. What's in it?"

"It's Canadian bacon, slice of tomato, poached egg with Hollandaise sauce on an English muffin."

"Sounds messy." Loretta grinned gleefully. "I'll have a ham and egg sandwich on wheat toast."

"Okay."

"Will we have to dig through them all to find our sandwich?"

"No. They usually are labeled with your name on the wrapping. Is coffee okay?"

"No. I want English breakfast tea with lemon."

"Okay. We can send someone to bring you down there."

"No, I'll go a bit early to get myself situated. How soon will the room be open?"

"About twenty minutes before the meeting. That allows time for the delivery man to get there before the group arrives."

"I'll go down then."

Loretta hung up and swirled her chair in a circle, "This will be a red letter day! I better go to the bathroom and then get down there. I wonder if I should take a lace kerchief along to dab Miss Diane's tears?"

The woman was absolutely jubilant and sang, *"When you are down and out, Lift up your head and shout, It's gonna be a great day!"*

Then she checked; her vodka was chilling, her clam juice was tucked carefully in an easily accessible place, her hair looked perfect and she carried her 'mourning' handkerchief.

She went out into the hall and pulled her door closed. Then she made her way toward the consulting room. She got there a few minutes before the delivery man. The lady from the front desk unlocked the room for him and smiled at Mrs. Berg.

"You must be hungry?"

"I've never been a fan of eating things wrapped in paper," Mrs. Berg snapped.

The delivery man smiled, "Then you must be looking forward to this meeting?"

"You have no idea, Sonny," the lady sneered. "None whatsoever."

"You still have fifteen minutes before the others arrive. Are you certain you want to wait here?" the girl checked.

"Yes, of course. Maybe I could ask you to open the glass door and let some air in?"

"I can do that."

The man put the sandwich box on the table and the girl set the tray with the coffee and tea on the sideboard. Then she opened the sliding door and let the spring breeze in. She asked Mrs. Berg if she wanted her to bring her some tea, but Loretta answered that she'd get it herself. She couldn't wait for them to leave.

Finally, the man and woman left her alone. The drapes to the hall were closed, the lights were on in the room and a fresh sea breeze circulated all the sandwich odors out of the room. She went to the box of sandwiches and looked for the one labeled Matt. When she found it, she carefully took it out of the box and unwrapped it. She had to hurry.

# 7

D r. Werner and the head nurse, Estelle Wainwright, were the first into the room. They were both surprised to see Mrs. Berg sitting there drinking her tea, looking as precious as a Hallmark card. "They brought you down early. I hope they didn't leave you sitting here too long?" Estelle asked.

"I came down myself and just made my tea. Haven't been here but a minute or so."

"Did you have any problems making it here?" Dr. Werner asked as he poured his coffee.

"It was tiring, but that is why I wanted to get here early. I needed time to get situated and rest up before the meeting."

The hall filled with other meeting attendees. Loretta's caseworker and the four family members arrived. Dr. Werner asked about Bea's cast and she explained it all to them. "You know it is wise to take the time to heal, even if it seems unnecessary. Dancing puts a lot of stress on the tibia and it needs to be strong. The only good cure of a tibia is resting the bone."

"I know, but I hate to miss so much practice." Bea explained, "The doctor for the ballet company is very good and will help me with exercises to keep fit until I can get back to dancing. Once I get my leg back, it will take a couple months to get back to where I was."

"I imagine. Does the company carry you that long?"

"Usually. My contract is good. After six months, I have to renegotiate. A person can't really expect more than that."

"I guess not. I hope it goes well," Dr. Werner said. "It could be a career-ender if not cared for properly."

"It could be anyway," Bea pointed out. "Six months out of practice is really pushing it."

Loretta feigned concern over Bea's crutches and apologized profusely. It was difficult for her to disguise her joy while carrying on, but she thought she managed it well. Estelle found her difficult to console, and was convinced the poor lady was beside herself. The family simply ignored her.

Then they all got their coffee and sat down. Loretta smiled to herself, noticing that all the kids sat as far away from her as possible. Loretta pretended not to notice.

Dr. Mason, one of the general physicians and head physical therapist came in and started rummaging through the sandwiches. "I hope everyone is hungry."

Werner laughed, "I know I am. I'll get your coffee, if you hand out the sandwiches."

"Good idea."

Dr. Mason carefully read each label and gave the sandwich to the correct person. Estelle handed out the paper plates that were also in the box. Dr. Werner smiled, "We can eat and then maybe begin our meeting."

Loretta watched as everyone opened their sandwiches and put them on their paper plates. There were many comments about how good they looked. A few sniffed their sandwiches and Loretta was glad that Matt didn't. However, he was sitting in front of the open sliding door, so he may not have been able to smell much anyway.

Loretta was anxiously waiting for the meeting attendees to bite into their sandwiches, but they had to go through a whole rigmarole of handing out napkins. Tolerating the distractions was keeping her nerves on edge.

Finally, everyone settled into eating. They were all chatting about Bea's cast and the length of Randy's tour of duty. He had decided not to re-enlist after this stint. He was planning to move to the Midwest and work as an air traffic controller there.

Matt seemed to be playing with his sandwich and hadn't taken a bite yet. Loretta was becoming extremely frustrated, thinking to herself, 'Why is he such a picky eater?'

Diane leaned over toward his sandwich, "Yours looks interesting. Aren't you hungry?"

"Yes, but not ravenous like you," he teased. "You can eat it if you want."

"I'll have a taste," Diane said as she picked up the sandwich.

She took a big bite and then set it back on his plate. She chewed the mouthful and smiled, "It is good. It has a unique flavor I haven't tasted before in Hollandaise, but it's good."

"Well, since my taste tester approved, I can dig in," Matt laughed and took the sandwich up to his mouth.

As he did, the tomato slipped out onto his plate. He put the sandwich back down and opened the English Muffin. Loretta's heart was in her throat.

Matt put the tomato back in place and then took a bite. He swallowed and took another bite. This bite had a lot of Hollandaise on it.

Within a couple seconds, he started to choke. He dropped his sandwich gasping to get air. He tried frantically to get his breath and was unable to. He pushed back from the table and fell back. He passed out onto the floor. Dr. Mason was right there and tipped his head so he didn't choke on the food in his mouth. Estelle took his pulse and gave Mason a worried look. Dr. Werner jammed a syringe filled with Epinephrine into Matt's thigh from the emergency medical cabinet in the room. He looked at the other two, "Working?"

Estelle nodded, "A bit. Should I make the call?"

Mason said, "Yes. I think he is getting little air."

Werner asked group, "Do you know anything he's allergic too?"

Diane answered, "Clams." Then realization spread on her face, "That was the taste in the sandwich!"

Bea frowned, "I never heard of putting clams in Eggs Benedict."

Bea pulled Matt's sandwich toward her and lifted the muffin. One sniff and she nodded. "That's what it is! Looks like clam juice all over the sauce!"

Randy glared at his mother who was dabbing her eyes with her lace handkerchief. He knew that look. Had he not needed to move to make room for the men with a stretcher, he would have killed her there. Instead, his attention went to Matt.

"Need to do a trach?" Werner asked.

"I think the oxygen will do it," Mason said. "Is the ambulance on it's way?"

"Four minutes out," one of the attendants answered. "Let's move him to the medical wing for pickup."

With that, they put Matt on the gurney and rushed him down the hall. Diane followed beside him while Randy helped Bea to her feet. As they were leaving the room, Loretta shook her head and thought to herself, 'They are so pathetically dumb.'

The caseworker helped a distraught Loretta back to her room and put her on her bed to rest. After an acceptable amount of worry and weeping, Loretta began to fall to sleep. The caseworker quietly moved out of the room.

Once Loretta heard the door close, she crawled out of bed and went to her wheelchair. There, she removed the empty bottle of clam juice from her scarf. She wrapped it in a paper towel and buried it in the bottom of her trashcan. Then she carefully put her scarf in her laundry bin and washed her hands very thoroughly. There was no slight odor of clams on her and what may have lingered was masked by the stench of perfume.

After a mighty swig of vodka, Loretta crawled back into her bed and smiled, "Ah, it was simply delightful. I thought that defrocked monk would never take that first bite." She scrunched up her nose, "That only added to the excitement!"

The woman sighed deeply, smugly grinned and fell sound asleep.

# 8

Diane rode with Matt in the ambulance while Randy and Bea followed in the Toyota. Alone in the car, Randy burst out to Bea, "I know she did it! She actually tried to kill him! I just pray he makes it. I almost wrung her neck then and there."

Bea was very serious, "Do you truly believe that?"

"Yes, Bea. I know it." Randy spoke gravely and evenly, but his hands were shaking. "I have no evidence or proof, but I know her look. I know she did it. What should we do?"

"Are you sure she even knew he was allergic to clams?"

"Yes, remember when he first came in yesterday? He told her. I can't remember how it came up."

Bea raised her eyebrows, "Yes! I do remember that. When they were talking about the soup, he said he was very allergic to clam chowder. How would she have done it? She had no access to clams."

"I intend to find out," Randy said as they pulled into the lot. "As soon as I can, I'm calling one of those doctors at Shorepoint."

Bea took his hand as he turned off the ignition. "Randy, what are you going to do about it; if she did this? You can't very well expect her to go to jail, could you?"

"I don't care if they hang her! She might have killed Matt. She tried to break your legs! She put your career in jeopardy. Diane almost went crazy last fall! She drove my Dad away and he died alone. That is enough that any one person should be allowed. Don't you think?"

"I agree, but please don't shout. You need to think this out and decide what should be done."

Randy leaned back in the seat, "I'm sorry I shouted. I didn't realize that I was talking so loud. I don't want the people I love to be hurt. Bea, I have to do something."

"Take a deep breath and think. Your Mom does nothing without putting a lot of thought into it. We won't be able to get ahead of her if we go off half-cocked."

Randy looked at her, "Does that mean you are with me?"

"Of course, I plan on spending my life with you. I had visions of it being a reasonably long life. If your Mom has her way, it might be a lot shorter than I'd like. We need to use our heads."

"God, I love you."

They shared a brief kiss before Randy helped her out of the car.

They found Diane shredding a tissue in her hands outside a waiting room with tears rolling silently down her face. When they came in, Diane stood up and buried her face in her brother's arms. Bea rubbed her back and then had her sit down.

Diane quit crying and then said, "Mom did it, didn't she?"

"We think so, Di." Randy squeezed her, "How is Matt doing?"

"I haven't heard yet. They are worried. They might have to intubate him and he ingested a lot of the allergen. His throat is closed. His bronchi are in spasm and respiration is sporadic. He hasn't been conscious since he was in the ambulance." Diane's tears came back, "Should I call his family?"

"Yes, but let's give it a few minutes to see if we have anything else to tell them. Okay? They couldn't get here in minutes anyway."

Diane sat staring into nowhere. "That's what I thought. You guys, I don't want to lose him. He is the only thing that makes sense in my life. I can't believe how many times I doubted him and pushed him away! He was always there and stood by me. I should've told him how much I appreciated him, but I didn't. I treated him like he would always be there, no matter what! I could just kick myself."

Bea hugged her, "Everyone does that, especially with those we count on. It doesn't make it right, but it's easy to do. I know that he loves you."

Randy knelt down next to her and teased, "Yah, I must have heard him talk about it a million times. I just figured he didn't know you very well."

A small smile broke through, and Diane said, "Bea, are you sure you want to marry this creep?"

"Ah, what the hell? I need some excitement in my life."

They sat silently for half an hour. A doctor came out, "Are you with Mr. Harrington?"

Diane stood up, "I'm Matt's fiancée. How is he?"

"He is hanging in there, but it's nip and tuck. Is there family here than can sign for him if he needs surgery?"

"No, they are in Boston. We were waiting to hear something before we called them. Will he need surgery?"

"Don't know," the scrub-clad man said. "We are shoving as much Epinephrine into him as his body can stand. We should know in another half an hour. You might want to wait until then to let his family know. I'll come back out as soon as I know or if I think you should call. Okay?"

By now, they were all standing, the doctor held out his hand, "I'm Dr. Kurts, by the way. And you are?"

"I'm Diane Waggoner. This is my brother, Randy Berg and his fiancée Bea Fedder."

"I thought I recognized you from this morning. You have a tibia, right?"

Bea smiled, "I do, and I believe you do too. But mine has a cast on it!"

"I deserved that." The doctor smiled, "I saw you in the waiting room. Better keep your leg up. Pull one of those chairs over here. Okay? I'm going back in and will let you know right away. Oh, what faith is he? In case something goes bad?"

Diane started to cry and Randy answered, "He is Roman Catholic."

The doctor put his hand on her shoulder and patted it. "I'll let you know."


Randy held his sister for a bit, consoling her. Then he said, "I can't stand it. I'm going to call the Shorepoint. Okay?"

"Okay," Bea said as Diane sat down. "You should do that. Try to keep calm when you talk to them."

Randy found a payphone and waited impatiently for the girl to get one of the Shorepoint doctors on the line. Dr. Werner answered and asked, "How is Mr. Harrington?"

Randy shared what he knew and the doctor concurred. "Sometimes it takes a lot to calm the respiratory distress. Let us know. I'm so sorry about this. I have to say, I find it odd that Sunrise Sandwich would use clam juice in a breakfast sandwich. I don't think that I have ever seen anything clam on their menu."

"I don't think they did."

"What do you mean?"

"I think Mom did it," Randy said matter-of-factly.

"What?"

"If I come over there, could I meet with you in private?"

"I'll wait for you. Just tell the receptionist that I'm waiting for you."

Randy walked over to where the girls were sitting, "Would you hate me if I went to talk to Werner now? I'll come right back. Somehow, it didn't seem right accusing my mother of attempted murder over the phone."

Just then, the door opened and Dr. Kurts came out. He smiled, "I have good news. We finally got enough dope in him to get his respiratory distress under control. He'll be sleeping for quite a while, but he is out of the woods. No surgery, no trach. He should emerge unscathed. It might take him up to 48 hours to work it out of his system."

"How soon will he wake up?" Randy asked.

"We're going to move him to a room in a few minutes. I'd think a couple of hours at least, and he will be quite groggy for a while."

"Can I stay with him?" Diane asked.

"Sure. You all can."

"Should I call his family?"

"You can call, but let them know the worst is past. He is on the mend. Okay?"

"Thank you."

The door opened and the attendants moved Matt's bed down the hall. Diane started to follow and then said, "You guys go talk to Werner. I'll be fine."

"Me, too?" Bea asked. "I can stay if you want."

"You keep a lid on Randy. Come back and tell me what you discover. Okay? I'll call his parents as soon as I get to a phone. I'm just telling them that he had an allergic reaction and not mentioning all this other business until we know more. Is that okay?"

Bea nodded, "Yes. That's what I'd do, until we at least know what we are talking about."

Diane called his parents in Boston while the attendants set Matt up in his room. She assured them they didn't need to interrupt their vacation and she would keep them informed. When she hung up, she went in to his room. She went to his bed where he was sleeping, tethered to his IV. She kissed him and touched his cheek. "I love you."

He slept on and she sat down in a nearby chair and watched him breath. While she said there, she began thinking about plans for their wedding. Even though she had not confronted her mother, she had put her into perspective. She knew for certain that she would never doubt Matt's trustworthiness or put any stock in her mother's opinion again!

# 9

Randy was very glad that Bea was with him. It gave him more confidence and credibility. At first, Randy thought Dr. Werner was a hard sell. Especially when he pointed out the Mrs. Berg had often said that her children always painted her in a bad light and many times just lied about her outright.

Werner's mind opened after his many discussions with Dr. Samuels during Diane's hospitalization, but as he explained, "I'm not a clinical psychiatrist, but I did study geriatric psychiatry. Your mother isn't really even geriatric. We all think of her as old but she is only 59. I think that is one source of frustration for her. She'd like to think that she is still a very attractive, vibrant woman."

"Well, if she'd get out of that damned chair, let her hair go back to the brown it always was and develop a few smile wrinkles, she might be. Gad, she looks so severe, she makes a vampire seem loveable," Randy stated emphatically.

"You don't like her very much, do you?"

"I hate her," Randy said without emotion, "Have for years. Let me tell you what she has done in just this last month."

Randy explained her entire behavior, including her cutting and insulting remarks. He explained about the clams and running into Bea with her wheelchair. Dr. Werner never said a word and Randy was beginning to think he needed to go to the police.

When he finished talking, Werner picked up the phone. "Before I tell you what I think, I need to take care of some things."

Randy was almost angry, but Bea took his hand. Dr. Werner listened while the phone rang and finally said, "Hello. I need some things from you immediately that are very important. Can I count on you?"

"Okay," he continued. "Has Loretta Berg's room been cleaned today?"

"Good. I want you to send someone now. Please act like it is usual, but seal the garbage bags and initial them with the time. I'd also like her laundry bag. Keep the things in the storage room. Clean her fridge and tell me what you find in it. We need to maintain a chain of custody the way we did when we had those robberies. Remember? Don't let on to Mrs. Berg there is anything out of normal."

Then he dialed the front desk, "Could I get a list of any calls or visitors in and out of Loretta Berg's room last night and today? Do you know who was working this morning? You were? Great. After you gather this information, I need to see you in person. Come to my office when you get someone to cover for you. Thank you, Marie."

Randy was visibly relieved that apparently Werner did have faith in his word. The doctor sat back in the chair. "We should hear something soon. Oh, maybe I need maintenance to check the consult room." The doctor gave a silly smile, "This is almost like Dragnet!"

After making his call, he said, "The reason I'd called the meeting with you and Diane originally was because of the many concerns about your mother. Her health is deteriorating. She won't even move most days, to the point of having to be fed. Some days she won't get out of bed and soils herself. Then she complains and screams like a harpy. Some of the staff think she does it on purpose, so they have to clean her.

"Her blood pressure is barely under control and we have to monitor her medication. After we discovered she was stockpiling some of her blood pressure meds, we watch until we know she has swallows it. Boy, that was the worst chewing out I ever had in my life! She was livid when we threw her stockpile away!

"When she gets distressed or doesn't get her way, she allows herself to get too worked up, hyperventilating, raging and throwing herself about. We have thought she might have a stroke on several occasions, or really hurt herself by slinging herself out of her wheelchair or bed. She purports to be fragile and weak. However, we've all been hit or gouged enough to know that she isn't. Of course, she has little muscle tone left because she won't exercise or even move if she can help it. We are rather certain that she can get around on her own. Some days, she comes out into the hall having showered, dressed and everything by herself. You can't do that if you are truly dependent. She uses her weakness to be pampered. It doesn't sound nice to say, but we have thought that for some time.

"When she was working with the physical therapist, she could do a lot. Dr. Mason was hopeful she would soon be able to walk on her own. He mentioned that she might soon be able to take her meals in the dining room with the other residents and she went ballistic! She refused to go back to physical therapy. She continues to have her meals delivered to her room.

"Psychologically, we have been getting many signals that your mother was becoming more irrational and losing control. We had several complaints from the workers. First, it was her constant insults, but we get that a lot. She is the worst of our eleven hundred patients. However, the severe pinches, punches and 'accidental' gougings are becoming more frequent and extreme. She loves it when someone is lifting her and she knows they can't drop her. It is like a sadistic game with her.

"She has no friends left. She used to have a very few that she visited with, but she had driven them all away. Mrs. Berg was forever starting fights among the patients, which often were totally in her imagination.

"We know she had some brain damage from the meningitis, but that wouldn't account for all her behavior. She is definitely conniving and quite cruel. In combination with being a narcissistic paranoid, she can be frightening. The things you've told me, don't surprise me at all.

"I guess I was being optimistic and hoped that she would be so delighted to see her daughter and have her whole family visit that things would get better. She talked incessantly about her 'only' son and 'only' daughter coming to see her and all the wonderful things you would do together. I have to say, I was shocked how she behaved when you were here.

"We were going to tell you we wanted you to find other accommodations for her. We can't have someone this disruptive here. The other residents avoid her like the plague and some of the staff refuse to help her.

"When we warned her, she almost seemed pleased. I wondered about it at the time. She told us that she didn't want to stay in this 'dump' and that you kids were going to buy her a home and care for her there. This sounds terrible to say, but we were hoping you would all get along and you would take her out of here!"

"Fat chance," Randy growled. "Hell, she would probably have half of us dead before the week was out."

Werner gave a disgusted nod, "If in fact she did do this, how do you think we should remedy this? Have her arrested, face a trial and all that? She'd be out of our hair, but you need to realize that she could be the most sympathetic defendant. I don't know if a jury would convict her. You would likely find it difficult to prove she intended to kill Mr. Harrington. She might have only thought he'd get a little sick. Unless I knew her, that's what I would assume. I wouldn't find her guilty of attempted murder . . . more like malicious mischief. Knowing her as I do, I think she intended to kill him and probably wanted to sever both Bea's legs off at the knees. I truly mean that. However, I doubt a jury could be convinced. It is too bad a person can't be convicted for what the damage they *intend*. I never thought a person should be given a lighter sentence because they were a lousy shot or the proximity of a good doctor!"

Randy leaned back in his chair, "I'm so glad you understand. I was afraid that you were on her side."

"I am, really." The doctor continued, "Mrs. Berg is not doing herself any favors. She has lost many years of a fulfilling life because of her behavior. I hope she hasn't messed up the rest of it. Most of the staff here are pretty patient and understanding. I hate to say it, but I would be hard put to find one that even wants to be around her."

"I can understand that," Randy nodded.

"Well, let's see what we find out. Then we make the decision on how to progress."

Matt started wheezing in his sleep and before long, coughed himself awake. He was confused when he opened his eyes and couldn't figure out where he was. It was difficult for him to keep awake more than a minute and was very drowsy during that time.

Diane moved to his bedside. The doctor had told her he would wheeze and cough a lot and probably be very hoarse for a couple days. She took his hand and touched his cheek, "Hello. How are you?"

He looked at her, "Where am I?"

"At St. Mary's hospital in Portsmouth, Maine."

He frowned trying to understand why he would be there, and Diane continued. "We were at Shorepoint and you had an anaphylactic reaction to your sandwich. You quit breathing and the doctors brought you here."

His eyes studied her for more explanation, "Where?"

"St. Mary's hospital. You're doing well now, but we almost lost you. Don't ever scare me like that again."

"Don't scare you," he whispered absently as he fell back to sleep.

Diane smiled and watched him while he lay there, wheezing with every breath. He was an amazing person. The youngest of eight children, he was raised mostly by his mother who was widowed when he was twelve. His father was a policeman who was shot in the line of duty. Everyone in the family made a career in law enforcement, but him. He became a priest.

He was a good priest and loved by his congregation in Boston. When a new priest moved into a nearby parish, Matt began hearing rumors that he was making obscene advances to some young boys. Several members from that parish came to talk to Matt about it. Once he was convinced the man was a pedophile, he reported it to the Bishop. Nothing was done and the misbehavior continued.

Matt reported the offender frequently but nothing was ever changed. After a year or so, Matt had become a thorn in the side of the Diocese. The Bishop placed him on suspension by the Bishop for being 'undisciplined'. He told Matt that he needed to accept the decisions made by the diocese about the matter. He needed to use the suspension as time to reconsider his vocation. That is when he decided to resign the priesthood.

Matt moved to North Dakota and took a temporary teaching job at the local high school. He lived in a small cabin on a friend's farm and earned his rent by helping Darrell and his wife with the milking. Jessups had a dairy, and milked over seventy goats and cows twice a day.

Meanwhile, Diane was working herself up to a nervous breakdown after the attempted rape and thrown down the stairs, but Matt stayed by her side. She knew she had been horrible to him more often than not, but he stood with her. She embarrassed him and purposely aggravated him, but he was there. He continued to love her and gave her every chance in the book. He was there with a forgiving, optimistic spirit; looking forward to having a regular life with her. She even pushed that off. She had accused him of just wanting sex, but he convinced her that was not it. He wanted her, she knew that; but he had been very respectful of her. Once he said, "I couldn't look in the mirror if I betrayed everything I taught all those years. You are very precious to me, and I want our marriage to reflect that."

She patted his hand, 'I can't believe that I worried so much about what my mother thought, I almost shunned this man. If Matt and Bea were smart they should tell both us kids to go away.'

Diane suddenly panicked. She put her hands to her face. "My God, what if he won't put up with this? What if he leaves me now? Nearly being murdered could do that. I wouldn't blame him a bit!"

Diane started crying harder and put her head in her hands. A minute later, she felt his hand on her arm. "What is it?" he asked hoarsely. "What's bothering my girl?"

Diane nearly fell into his arms and put her head into his shoulder. He wrapped his free arm around her and whispered, "It's okay. I promise. I love you."

"I love you, too."

"There, there," he patted her back and then fell back to sleep.

Diane straightened up and regained control. "I hope so, Matt. I really hope so."

She sat down and started to worry again. Realizing she was getting herself wound up, she took a deep breath. This time, Matt needed her to be strong. She was determined not to let him down. She also was aware that she couldn't do it alone. Bea had her hands full with Randy. She shouldn't interrupt them.

She went to the payphone in the hall and dropped her coins into the slot. She called Dr. Samuel's office. The receptionist got the number for the phone there and said she would have him call her right back. It was a few minutes before the phone in the hallway rang. Diane answered it quickly.

Dr. Samuels said, "Hello Diane. What can I do for you?"

Diane just babbled out the information as simply as she could and tried to keep her tears contained. There was silence on the line. Diane wondered if the connection had been broken. Then he said, "How are you holding up?"

"Pretty wobbly, as Elton would say."

"I think you are doing pretty well. Matt would be proud of you."

Through tears, Diane said softly, "Thank you. I hope so."

"Are you taking your pills?"

"Matt has been giving them to me. You told him I shouldn't take them myself. He has them in his motel room."

"When are you due for the next ones?"

"I took one before we went to the meeting, that was about three hours ago."

"Could you have Randy get them for you? I need you to keep taking them regularly so you have that security. Can you contact him?"

"Yes, I have to admit, I'm getting pretty shaky. Dr. Samuels, do you think that Matt will leave me after Mom tried to poison him?"

"Diane, I doubt that very much. Try to keep calm. Think about it. Did Bea leave Randy?"

"No, but Mom only tried to cripple her!"

Samuels couldn't help it and started to laugh. Then Diane realized how ridiculous that sounded and started to laugh, too. "Yea gads, Dr. Samuels. What am I saying?"

Samuels chuckled, "I've always said insanity is contagious! Okay, here's what we'll do. If you can't get in touch with Randy, call me back and I'll call Matt's doctor to have him get you one to tide you over. Okay?"

"Okay."

"When he wakes up, tell him hello for me. He can call when he's more awake, if he would like. Randy can, too. In fact, I have a better idea. I'll call Dr. Werner and talk to him. He can talk to Randy and ask him to get your pills. I'd also like to find out how they are doing. Do I have your permission?"

Diane giggled, "Now tell me the truth. Are you doing this because I'm your patient or because you are nosy?"

Samuels chuckled, "Because I'm nosy, of course. I'll call Werner now and if you don't hear from Randy within half an hour, call me back. Okay?"

"Here is the number to Matt's room for when you call back. Then I won't have to stand in the hallway. Thank you."

The phone rang in Dr. Werner's office while he was talking to Bea and Randy. He excused himself and answered it. "Of course, put him through."

"Hello Dr. Samuels. I'm here with Randy Berg and his fiancée Bea at this moment. May I put you on speaker phone?"

The four talked together for about twenty minutes. They all agreed that if the facts were as they felt they were, the police needed to be notified. Even though nothing may come of it, liabilities needed to be covered and the behavior needed to be documented for any future activities on her part.

When they hung up, Randy and Bea left for the motel to get Diane's medication. Dr. Werner was going to call the police.

When they came down the hall at the hospital, they saw Diane coming out into the hall heading for the phone. "I'm here," Randy waved. "No need to call Samuels again."

Diane smiled, "Good. I wasn't going to. I thought I'd call Werner."

"Anyway, I picked up your pills and Bea's," Randy chuckled. "I almost feel left out!"

Bea raised her eyebrow and poked, "Maybe we could arrange for you to spend the afternoon with your Mom. By nightfall, you will be on something!"

"Yah," Diane nodded. "What did Werner think?"

Randy and Bea filled Diane in on their meeting with Werner while she took her pill. They all went to sit in Matt's room. Bea asked, "How has he been?"

"Wheezing, coughing and very sleepy. Poor guy can hardly keep his eyes open," Diane explained.

Randy chuckled, "Keeps his mind off his crotch."

That drew a whack from both women and he retorted, "Well, I bet it does. Did you tell him what she did?"

"He doesn't stay awake that long." Diane pointed out. "How's your leg? Should you have it up?"

"I had it up in Werner's office, but I really should lie down. It's beginning to ache a lot," Bea said.

"Honey, would you like to go back to the room?" Randy asked. "You could have a nap and then I could pick you up when you wake."

"I should, but you can't be running back and forth with me when all this is going on."

"Why don't you sit in that big chair in Matt's room? It is almost a recliner," Diane explained. "You could sleep there."

Randy frowned, "How can something 'almost' recline?"

"I think we are getting punchy!" Diane said and they all laughed.

That woke Matt and Diane went to him, "Hi."

"Hi. I want to go home," Matt said groggily.

Randy went to him, "Can't Man, you have to stay until the doctor's say you can leave. You almost croaked on us. You're really allergic to clams."

Matt frowned, "Clams?"

"There was clam juice on your sandwich," Randy explained. "You went out in no time."

"I don't eat clams," Matt mumbled and dozed off.

Randy patted his shoulder, "No you don't."

Matt opened his eyes again, "Randy, Diane's pills in suitcase."

"Already got them. Don't worry," Randy said. "I got it covered."

Matt nodded, "Covered."

He went back to sleep.

Bea was settled in the recliner, "Why don't you hand me that throw blanket and then you two go back to Shorepoint? I can keep an eye on Matt and rest here with my leg up."

Randy covered her up, "Sure you'll be okay?"

She kissed his cheek, "If you keep me informed. Now go, you are disturbing Matt and I want to snooze."

Randy chuckled. Diane kissed Matt goodbye. He opened his eyes and put his arm around her. "Want to make out?" Then he fell back to sleep.

Randy shook his head, "We know where his mind is! Come on Sis. These guys might lead us astray."

"Now that would take some doing," Bea giggled.

# 10

Randy and Diane followed a couple into Shorepoint Care Center. When they stopped at the front desk, Marie, the receptionist pointed out they were all there on the same matter and she accompanied them down the hall. Marie knocked on Werner's door and he told her to come in. Werner offered his hand to the police who introduced themselves.

"I'm Detective Michael Eastman," the tall, young police officer said as he shook Dr. Werner's hand. "This is Detective Flo Lauer."

Dr. Werner shook the matronly detective's hand. "Mrs. Lauer."

"Detective Lauer," The short lady clarified. "So, you folks think intrigue is lurking the halls of your nursing home?"

"This isn't a nursing home, and yes, we think we have a patient who may not have succeeded, but would certainly wanted to do away with a few folks," Werner stated. "Sit down and we'll tell you what we know."

It was only a brief explanation of events and the gathering of the trash from her room and the consult room. Det. Eastman labeled the bags and set them aside. "We'll take them back to the station. Where is Mrs. Berg now?"

"In her room," Werner replied.

"Alone?"

"Yes."

"Who are these people and what's their connection?" Det. Lauer asked brusquely.

"I'm Randy Berg, her son and this is my sister, Diane Waggoner."

"I'm Marie Johnson and I work at the front desk. I'm here because Dr. Werner asked me to gather a list of Mrs. Berg's guests and phone calls from last night and this morning."

"Good," Flo Lauer decreed with an authority she could well have learned in a Soviet Gulag. She looked like she could pin a Sumo wrestler with one hand tied behind her back. "Well, Det. Eastman can talk to you, Marie and take your statement. Werner, you got a private place handy?"

"Certainly, you can use a couple consult rooms."

"Okay, show us the way," Det. Lauer stood up her whole five foot-three inch height with her notebook already open and motioned for Randy to follow her. "Randy Berg. You can tell me your story."

Diane and Dr. Werner were left sitting in his office. After the door closed, they looked at each other seriously, and then broke into laughter. "My word! I wouldn't want her to catch me with my hand in a cookie jar!"

"Me either," Werner laughed. "Bet she knows what she's doing though."

"I think so."

"So, how is your young man doing?"

Diane explained his condition. Dr. Werner reassured her that he would likely be waking up more in a few hours. Then they made small talk until the detectives came back.

Detective Eastman looked over the information Marie had gathered. "It looks here like she called a grocer and had several things delivered this morning. Is that usual?"

"She ordered things from time to time. Not on a regular basis," Marie answered. "I called the grocer and he gave me the name of the delivery boy this morning. Here is his name and phone number. He's a nice kid. When he came out past the desk this morning, he said, "She actually gave me a two dollar tip! I should have it mounted! She's never given me more than a dime before—followed by a complaint call to my boss! I can hardly wait to get back to the store to hear what she had to complain about this time!"

The detective put the paper in his notebook, "I will call there. Was it his boss who took the order?"

"Yes, that's his number. Mrs. Berg isn't a very nice lady. No one likes her," Marie stated.

"Was she so unpleasant that people would make up stuff to get her into trouble?"

"No. I mean she is that bad, but you know how sometimes people are so rotten they aren't worth the effort? That is her." Maria thought, "I truly doubt anyone would think it was worth it to try to get her into trouble. She was good enough at that herself."

"It seems that you let her into the room almost twenty minutes before the meeting and then left her alone in there? Is that normal?"

"No, she usually had to have someone take her down there, but we have never monitored someone while they were waiting for a meeting to start unless they had serious health issues."

They talked a bit more and then Det. Eastman gave her his card. "If you think of anything else or need to change something, call me. I'll have this typed up and ready for you to sign by tomorrow. Will you be working?"

"Yes, same time. You have my home number too, right?"

"I do." The young detective shook her hand. "Thank you for your time."

Marie left for the day and Det. Eastman returned to Werner's office. "I guess I should speak to you, Ms. Waggoner. Okay?"

Diane followed the lanky man out of the room.

The middle-aged detective looked around the consult room as she and Randy sat down for his statement. "Nice place. Are the rooms this nice?"

"Nicer," Randy said. "This is a good care center."

Detective Lauer nodded, "Pricey, I bet. Is it a burden on you kids to keep your Mom here?"

"Not really. Mom gave us power of attorney a long time ago to take care of her," Randy explained. "We sold our house and put the money in a trust to keep her here. I sent money all the time, but Di only did after she got out of college. Then last year, after Diane's nervous breakdown, we found out that Mom had a humungous safe deposit, stuffed with bonds from Dad's life insurance policy. She had neglected to mention that to us."

"So, I bet you kids had a party then, huh? After all those years of doling out for her?" the detective probed.

"No. We put that into the trust to take care of her. You need to know her background to understand," Randy leaned back in his chair.

"That's what I'm here for. Lay it out, because all I have now is a frail, little old lady who is rather nasty. She has become difficult and expensive to take care of and her kids want to get rid of her."

Randy grunted, "I guess it sounds that way. First off, she is only 59 years old."

Detective Lauer's eyes popped open, "I'm only a year younger! She must have had some bad health."

"That's when it all started," Randy began. "There was Dad, Mom, Di and me. We had a regular life. When I just turned fifteen, Mom got meningitis. She almost died. She ended up with brain damage, mostly motor skills and personality. Physically she was very weak. Then everything went to hell."

"How old was Diane then?"

"Twelve."

"So, this is as fit as she will ever be?"

"No. Let me continue," Randy said. "She came home for the hospital and we all catered to her. She had been a good person up 'til then. Within a few months, she turned into a shrew. She was always whining, complaining, haranguing, and manipulating. She liked being waited on and wanted to be. She had us do everything from clean her ears to dress her. And she criticized us the entire time."

"A true bitch."

"Yes, and nothing seemed to help. She twisted Dad around so badly there was nothing that poor man could do. Eight months after she had come home from the hospital, he went to work one morning and never came home. She told us he walked out on us and we weren't allowed to say his name in her presence again. But mostly, she used it. Once he was gone, she demanded that we do everything for her. Diane and I cooked, cleaned, bathed her and I mean everything. It was constant. We weren't allowed any activities outside of school except music. She had the teachers come to the house for lessons, and then she had us entertain her. Any time we were interested in something away from home, she destroyed it."

"How did she do that? She's in a wheelchair."

"Telephone, lying, manipulation, trickery."

Randy went on to explain what she did with the laxative at the track meet and putting Diane's necklace in the kitty litter. She shook her head, but her expression was difficult to read.

"So you don't like her very much," the detective said. "You have set yourself up with some great motivation to get her out of your hair."

"I despise her and I have for years. I won't lie about it. When Diane had a nervous breakdown last year, her psychiatrist asked to speak to Mom to get background. She refused. Finally, he arranged a medical emergency leave for me from the Air Force. I flew to North Dakota from overseas. It only took a short time for everyone to realize that while some of Diane's problems were from the man who tried to rape her, the major problem was when she started talking to Mom again."

"Why did she call your Mom?"

"The hospital did. She had been thrown down a stairs and had a concussion. They needed permission from next of kin and called Mom."

"Guess Diane was lucky she gave permission."

"She wasn't paying for it and everyone fussed over her. Mom played the poor invalid mother whose daughter was ill. That's what Mom likes the best. To be the center of sympathetic attention! Anyway, after Diane got out of the hospital, Schroeders, where she went to recover, and Matt thought she should let her Mom know she was okay and where she could be reached. Well, Diane got better physically, but talking to Mom turned Diane into a nervous nut bag."

"Over the phone?"

"Yah. Mom has a way of coming at us kids with first the guilt and the how self-sacrificing she is and ending on how we are worthless and need to fulfill our responsibilities to take care of her."

Detective Lauer tapped her pencil on the desk, "So you guys got together and concocted this plan to show her where the bear got into the buckwheat."

Randy chuckled, "You think you got that all figured out, huh? Well, we didn't. We just wanted to be as far away from her as possible, but she is our mother. Dad is gone. You know what she did? She told us that Dad skipped and then committed suicide. While Diane was in the hospital, on a conference call, Mom admitted that not only did she have all this money, but she had known where Dad was all the time. He never left Portland and sent her money for our care. He watched our graduation and such from a distance."

"Portland isn't that big. Why did you never run into each other?"

"Neither of us kids drove. We only went to the school, church and the doctor's office. There is no way we would have had a chance to run into him. When I got my license, I was only allowed the keys to the car when she was in it!"

"What about dating?"

"There was none. When I was about seventeen, Mom started to make sexual overtures to me, and ended up grabbing me every chance she got. I avoided being physically close to her."

"Did you tell anyone?"

"No. She would have lied her way out of it and I was embarrassed. I only admitted it the other day for the first time. It isn't something a guy wants to broadcast."

"Who did you tell? Is that when you decided to try to pin your Mom with attempted murder?"

Randy shook his head in despair, "She will worm her way out of this again. We should've just let her break Bea's legs and maybe kill Matt. Hell, she would still get out of it. It makes my head want to blow up! She manages to come out smelling like a rose, no matter what! Then you ask me why I never told anyone? It would have been just like this! I give up."

"Look, I have a job to do. I cannot just take everything everyone says at face value. You wouldn't want me to take your Mom's word for all this. Now, would you?"

"You won't question her. She will get all wimpy whiny and end up with some kind of damned medal for being a saint. I know how it works."

"Settle down. It has been a long day. I do have a few more questions. May I ask them?

"Knock yourself out."

Detective Lauer chuckled, "Okay, I will. So, what prompted you after all these years to spill the beans and to whom? Your fiancée?"

"No, to Matt, Diane's fiancé. He's a hell of a nice guy. When we took Mom to dinner, he sat next to her because we didn't trust her near Bea. While we were eating, she first made a pass at him by fondling his crotch. Then when he made it clear to her he wanted her to stop—"

"Excuse me, where were you people while this was going on?"

"We were at the salad bar and there was a long table cloth."

"Where did you eat?"

"The Angus Room."

"Nice place and they do have long tablecloths."

"Well, later she gouged him and nearly crippled him. He went to the rest room and I followed because I didn't think he looked good. He told me what happened and was worried about telling me something like that about my mother. That's when I told him that I understood because she had done it to me."

Detective Lauer nodded, "Then what?"

"I went out, moved her from the table and took her back here. Last night, we talked about how four perfectly fit young people were brought to our knees by this little woman."

"We should send her to Vietnam, huh?" Lauer looked over her notes, "Just a few more things. Did she know that Mr. Harrington was allergic to clams? And what his reaction was?"

"She knew he was extremely allergic to them, but not the reaction."

"So, she could have just wanted to give him a rash or diarrhea, like the track meet?"

"I guess that's possible. But she did it on purpose."

"Being a miserable person is not a crime. The prisons are overflowing as it is," Lauer smiled grimly. "Now, Bea's legs. Do you really think she wanted to break them?"

"Yes, beyond all doubt."

"That is difficult to do."

"She drove that wheelchair directly into her shins as fast as she could! She did manage to crack one bone. Bea is a ballerina with the New York City Ballet. Her career is now in jeopardy because of this and Mom knows it. She told me that she would make certain that Bea and I would never get married."

"She did? I must say, Bea must really love you. I almost didn't marry my husband because his mother told me how fat I was!"

"You aren't fat." Randy grinned, "I would call you cuddly."

Detective Lauer laughed, "And I would say you are full of it."

"Oh and so you know, Diane and I have decided to turn the trust fund over to a trust officer so we no longer have any responsibility or say over it. We don't want to ever have anything to do with her again. Period. It's bad enough she has tried to make us crazy, but we won't allow her to hurt the ones we love."

"It might not be that easy. I'll have this statement typed up and you will need to sign it. If the DA thinks there is enough to charge her, you will have to testify. Testifying against your mother, no matter how you feel about her, is difficult."

"I don't know about Diane, but I would do it."

"Well, I can't think of anything else this minute. I have your phone number and want to talk to some other folks. Here is my card. If you think of anything else, call Mike or me. Where will you be?"

"Either the hospital or motel. Bea needs to get some rest for her leg."

"Okay. Thank you for your time." Detective Lauer stood, "Let's get back to Werner."

# 11

Loretta Berg got out of bed and into her chair a few minutes before the cleaning people knocked on her door. She opened it and snapped, "About damned time you sloths showed up! I thought you'd never clean this dump! What is lunch today? I'm starving! I didn't get any breakfast!"

"It should be here soon," the man said, "Doreen, will you go check if Mrs. Berg's lunch is ready yet?"

The young girl with him disappeared out the door, "I will."

A few minutes later, she returned with a lunch on a tray. "Where would you like me to put this?"

Loretta rolled her eyes, "Over at the table by the window, you cretin. Where do they hire you people?"

The couple cleaned as quickly as possible while attending to Mrs. Bergs every whim; such as more salad dressing, lemon for the ice water and a new napkin because the first one was wrinkled. When Doreen cleaned out her refrigerator, she saw the lemons. "Mrs. Berg, did you remember you had fresh lemons in here?"

"Yes, I did. They are mine. I pay for my lunch and that includes lemons. You leave your mitts off my lemons, unless you want me to report you."

Doreen almost snapped back but Cal caught her glance and shook his head no. She turned back to her work.

A few minutes later, the couple finished cleaning. "Is there anything else, Ma'am?" Cal asked politely.

"Nothing you are capable of handling. Doreen dear, have you had training enough to take this tray out with you? Let the chefs know this was by far one of the worst lunches they have ever produced."

"I will pass that along, Mrs. Berg." Doreen said. "Have a nice afternoon."

"Hey, did my spoiled brats come back yet?"

"If you mean your son," Cal nodded, "I believe he is speaking with Dr. Werner."

"They'll probably be down here soon, begging my forgiveness."

"Yes Ma'am," Cal answered as they went out the door.

Mrs. Berg turned on the news, but couldn't concentrate. She was becoming anxious.

She wondered why no one had notified her of Matt's death. Then she decided they were all too busy sniveling around about it. Those kids always moved at a snail's pace. It might take them a while to come to her. She picked up a crossword puzzle.

Bea fell asleep but woke when she heard Matt coughing. She opened her eyes to find him fidgeting with his hands. She limped over to him and asked if he wanted something.

"Rosary?" Matt asked hoarsely.

"I can get it for you. Where is it?"

"Jacket."

Bea went to his clothing and found his jacket. She looked in his pockets and found his rosary made of wooden beads. She put his things back in the cupboard and brought it back to him. He was asleep again. She put the worn rosary into his free hand and closed his hand around it.

He looked at her, "Thanks. How's the leg?"

"It's much better," Bea smiled. "I've been sleeping here in your chair. How are you?"

Matt looked around and then shrugged before he fell back to sleep.

Bea smiled and patted his hand, "I'll be right over here if you need me."

He opened his eyes again, "Did I eat clams?"

Bea took his hand, "Not on purpose. There was clam juice in the sauce."

"Oh," Matt nodded. "Thanks for staying with me."

"No problem."

Diane and the young detective sat in one of the smaller conference rooms. After taking their seats, Detective Eastman began. He asked about her family life and childhood. She explained what had happened with her Mom's illness and her father. She told how her brother enlisted in the Air Force to get away from her demanding mother. When Diane got her scholarship for college, she and Randy had moved their Mom to the care facility while he was home on leave. They sold the house and used the money to finance her care. Diane stayed in the dorm.

She met Dean at college and they began dating, without letting her mother be aware. When she married, Diane never told her mother until after the ceremony. After the small civil ceremony, Diane had gone alone to see her. She told her that she was married and moving to North Dakota. She promised she'd write and send money to help keep her in Shorepoint. Loretta Berg became hysterical and threatened all sorts of horrible things. Diane left after the staff physician had sedated her mother.

Consequently, she had only extremely limited communication with her Mom or brother during that period of time. Their relationship was severely strained. Most of Diane's letters were returned and she had no more than three notes from her mother in that first year. She had almost lost track of Randy. Then Dean died. Once Diane was living with Waggoner's, she had even less communication.

She briefly explained about her marriage, Dean's death and his abusive parents, adding, "My psychiatrist pointed out that probably because of Mom's controlling and abusive nature, I never picked up on the signals about the Waggoners. Dean was in a very similar situation with his family."

Eastman nodded, "That happens. When did you see a psychiatrist?"

Diane explained about the beating and rape. She told him how she didn't get therapy when it first happened, but went to live at Schroeder's to physically recover. The hospital had notified Mrs. Berg that her daughter had been hospitalized, and Matt and Schroeder's felt Diane should call her Mom to tell her she was doing better.

That is when her mother started in on her. The woman worked tirelessly to destroy Diane's relationship with Schroeders and break up her and Matt. She also methodically chipped away at her sense of well-being, self-confidence and stability. Before long, she had managed to fill Diane with so much guilt and self-doubt that Diane ended up in the hospital with a nervous breakdown. Then Mrs. Berg refused to speak to Diane's doctors.

Diane smiled, "However, it turned out to be a good thing. My doctor called the Air Force and brought Randy to see me on an emergency medical leave. We were not only able to rebuild our relationship, but he also met Matt. They are great friends. And," she giggled, "That is when he met Bea. They are engaged to be married now."

"Is that the lady that Mrs. Berg attempted to break her legs?"

"Yes. She ran directly in to her, full speed. It was not an accident. She stated more than once that she hates Bea and that she will not allow her and Randy to marry. Of course, she hates Matt also, and thinks I shouldn't marry him."

Detective Eastman asked quizzically, "What does she want? Do you know?"

"Yes. Randy and I both know. She wants us kids to move here, buy a house and take care of her at home. She wants us to care for her like we used to when we had to cut her nails, trim her hair and everything. She didn't do anything for herself. It dawned on me the other day, that she wasn't happy then either! She complained constantly and criticized us. I don't think I could take it anymore. I'd have to kill myself."

Detective Eastman studied her, "Or her? It sounds to me as if you children do not want any part of her. You seem motivated to see her in jail. Could that be the case?"

"I really don't care what happens to her as long as she stays away from Randy and me. On the way over here today, we decided that we are contacting a lawyer and getting the trust out of our name assigned to some trust officer. They can pay for her care."

"What happens when the money runs out?"

"She can go live in an alley for all I care. If she would try, she could walk and get around. She just wants to be waited on. My god, if I had a nickel for every time I had to brush her teeth, I'd be a rich woman!"

"Brush her teeth? She must really be feeble."

"No, she's not. She thinks she is royalty or something and doesn't have enough self-respect to even clean herself."

"Do you know that she knew that Matt was allergic to clams?"

"Yes, the first day we arrived we were talking about clam chowder and Matt said he was extremely allergic to clams. So, the first thing she did is ask that we go to the Calm Shell for dinner! Randy and I both knew better than to do that without even talking about it!"

"It doesn't sound to me like she was plotting a devious scheme, if she was that open about going to the Clam Shell. Maybe it was a sad co-incidence."

"Yah right, and I climbed Mt. Everest this afternoon! If you only knew her and that look she gets. It is a smug, self-satisfied smirk that lets you know that she got her vengeance and there isn't a damned thing you can do about it."

"Well, I have a lot here and Detective Lauer and I need to talk to several others. Here is my card, if you can think of anything else. You are staying in town?"

"Yes. We were going to leave today, but this happened. Bea is on medical leave from the ballet, but Randy has to contact the Air Force and I need to call Matt's family. We have to extend our stay. That is obvious. How long do you think you'll need us here?"

"We don't know yet. Tomorrow at least, but then Mr. Harrington is still in the hospital. We have to speak to him and Bea Fedder. We will get these statements typed up and have you sign them tomorrow. We should have a better idea by then if there will be charges pressed."

"Okay, thank you," Diane said as she stood. "I know you may not believe it, but Randy and I really aren't figuring out how to dump our Mom. We could have done it years ago if that was what we wanted. We only wanted a normal family. Now we realize that a relationship with Mom cannot be normal or even safe. We have to get away."

"I understand," Detective Eastman nodded. "We will try to get this expedited as soon as possible. Thank you for your time."

Diane and Randy left Shorepoint for the hospital. At the first stop light, Diane finally broke the silence. "In my whole life, I never imagined we would be doing this!"

Randy nodded, "Me either. Di, I'm so glad you're my sister. You've always been there for me."

"You too. Will you get an extended leave?"

"I called my CO from Werner's office and I have the rest of the week. You better call Harringtons."

"I want to see Matt first. I need to call Nora and Elton too," Diane said. "I so wish they were here."

"Poor Mom," Randy said sarcastically. "She envisions herself as mother of the year. The dumb broad has no idea what that even is!"

"Randy, I got the definite feeling that Detective Eastman thought we might be trying to set Mom up."

"Yah, me too. But Lauer explained that they have to look at it from all angles."

"What a hell of a mess."

# 12

The siblings entered Matt's room and found their betrothed sleeping; Bea in the chair and Matt in his bed. They looked so peaceful and relaxed, Randy nudged Diane back to the door. "Let's go talk to his nurses and then make some phone calls before we disturb them."

"Good idea. They both need rest."

They learned from the nurses' station that Matt was doing very well and his IV was being cut back. He should be able to maintain without it soon and then he would be more awake. They felt it would be about another hour. The nurse directed them to a small alcove, where they could sit and make long distance phone calls. There was an hourly fee and worth every penny.

Randy called Bea's family in Vermont. Mrs. Fedder was very concerned about Bea's career and Diane's young man. "I shouldn't say anything, but Bea's father and I will be very pleased if all connections with your mother are cut. I know that sounds harsh, but we don't want our daughter or you subjected to all this misery."

"I agree. Diane and I are making every effort to divorce ourselves from any connection to her," Randy said. "I don't want Bea's life ruined over her. Trust me. I love her too much. You feel free to say what you want about the situation. I've talked to you both about my Mom. I doubt there isn't anything that you could say that I haven't thought myself."

"I know, Randy. Ben and I understand. We love you as our own. I hope you know that."

"I do, Madge, and I love you, too. I promise I will take the best care of Bea that I can. She is a saint."

Madge Fedder giggled, "I know her better than that, but her heart is in the right place. If you kids need Ben or me to come down, let us know. Thanks for calling. Could I ask that you call us tomorrow when you know the direction this will take? If you kids can get away, come to White River. Your sister and her beau are welcome, too."

"Thank you. I will ask Bea. Diane and Matt have to get back to North Dakota. They have school on Tuesday. It was kind of you to think of them. I'll let them know. Love you guys. Bye."

Diane watched her brother, "They sound like wonderful people."

"They are Di. I wish our family had been like that."

Diane took his hand, "Nora told me once that we can't change that, but we can appreciate a good family and build our own."

"I want that so much." Randy hugged his sister, "Who is next?"

"I should call Harringtons and Schroeders. Randy, could I ask you to explain all this legal business to them?"

"Sure, I'll be right here."

Diane dialed North Dakota. They figured that Elton should be home from work, but not our doing chores yet. It rang and within three rings, Nora answered.

"Hello, Nora," Diane said and then started to cry, "I love you."

"What is it Diane? Is everything okay?" Nora worried.

"It really sorta is. I'm at the hospital with Randy. Is Elton home?"

"He just got in. Do you need to talk to him?"

"Could he pick up the other phone too, so we can tell you everything at once?"

"Certainly, let me tell him."

Randy put their phone on speaker and soon they were all on line at once. "What is going on?" Elton asked. "Start at the beginning."

Randy and Diane explained everything that happened. Nora gasped a few times and Elton swore a little. Finally, he said, "At least everything is under control at this minute. How are you guys doing?"

"You'd be proud of my sister! She is holding up well," Randy boasted.

"Elton, I was interviewed by a policeman and didn't lose it! I guess I am turning into a real Bonnie!"

"Look girl, we weren't talking murder and mayhem when we talked about Bonnie and Clyde. That's my girl," Elton chuckled. "So, how is the investigation going?"

Randy explained they both felt that the detectives projected the feeling that *their* motives were in question and that *they* might be trying to 'set up' their mother.

Elton came unglued, "Sometimes I'd like to shake folks; but I guess they have no way of knowing. With your permission, I'd like to call Byron. I think I might need a preacher to get through this!"

"You can tell anyone. I would like it if you would talk to Bart. He'll be a basket case," Randy suggested. "We're calling Carl and Mo when we hang up here. I imagine Carl and Ian will be in the car heading our way before we hang up."

"Yah, would that help?"

"I don't think so. Detectives Lauer and Eastman seem on the ball and might resent any interference from retired law enforcement."

"Tell Carl that," Elton insisted. "I'm sure he would do what is best. He'd be there in a heartbeat if he thought he could help, but he wouldn't want to mess up the situation. May I ask; what outcome do you want?"

Diane answered, "We don't know. I'd hate to have my mother in jail, but that is what she deserves. Dr. Werner said he doubts that will happen. I just want her away from us."

Nora agreed, "I understand. You kids take care of Bea, Matt and yourselves. We don't want to lose any of you. I pray that Bea's leg heals so she can get back to the ballet before long. It would be a fright if her career was ruined by this nonsense! I should come out there and tell those detectives what I think of her! Loretta Berg has no right messing with my little chicks!"

Randy chuckled, "Thanks, Mom."

"I mean it. Well, call us when you can and please know you are in our thoughts."

Elton agreed, "I'll call Bart when we hang up and please let Matt and Bea know we love them. What does Matt think of all this?"

"He was furious about Bea's leg, but he doesn't know yet that Mom was the one responsible for giving him the clam juice."

"Good Lord, can you imagine Mo when she hears. If I was Loretta, I'd be scared to death!" Nora exclaimed.

The couple hung up and then Diane called Harringtons. Luckily, they were all at Matt's grandparents. As predicted, Carl and Ian went right through the roof, Ruthie started to pray and Mo went into orbit. She was immediately ready to head to Maine and give Loretta the what for. Carl got her calmed down and then she cried.

After the initial outburst, Carl and Ian were both rather objective. "You guys will play hell getting a case against her," Ian pointed out. "It is all circumstantial and could easily be excused as accidental or simply a prank of bad taste."

Carl was concerned that if the case was even charged; that she would get any jail time. "You need to realize that even if she was convicted, she might get little or no time. She is an invalid and therefore most people consider her sympathetically. If it was me, I would likely think the same way as those detectives. I'd wonder if you guys just didn't want to be burdened with her. I know better, but just saying."

"Me too," Ian concurred. "If you want, Dad and I can be there tonight. We can leave in half an hour."

"I know and thanks, but I doubt it would do anything but mess up your vacation. Matt is doing well, Bea has her cast and with any luck, Diane and I will sign our responsibility away in the morning. We want to leave the money with a trust officer or something. We just need to get out of here!"

"I'm having Carl bring me out there right now!" Mo blustered. "I have to see my Mattie and I don't need no cop! I'll slap that gargoyle witch into a paste! Just let me at her!"

"Mom," Diane said. "No. I don't want you to get into trouble over the likes of her. I give you my word. I'll take care of your son. He should be more awake in a couple hours and I will have him call you, okay? You are the best, but you might end up in the slammer and she'd be out!"

"Lord and the Host of Angels!" Mo exclaimed, "My little Diane is getting her back up! Good girl! I will let you have at it! But remember, you need a bit of help and I'd take great joy in being there! I'd appreciate the opportunity to—shall I say it? Take my shillelagh and smack the shit out of her!"

Everyone gasped and yelled, "Mom!"

"Leapin' Leprechauns, Mighty Mo," Carl embraced his wife. "Settle down. You need Ruthie to drag you off with your prayer beads and calm down."

"Why are you all yelling at me? I bet no one yells at that she-devil!" Mo muttered.

Ruthie got on the line, "Give everyone my love. I'm taking Maureen in the other room for meditation with the help of a roll of duct tape. Love you."

Carl took the phone, "We'll stay put and you call in. You need us even a little bit, we will be there."

"Thanks."

When they were walking back to Matt's room, Randy chuckled, "When you and Matt reproduce, it will be scary!"

Diane turned and frowned at him, "Why do you say that?"

"If your children inherit their temperament from either grandmother, they will be something else."

Diane punched her brother, "Or they could be nice like Matt and me!"

"Oh my, that makes me feel sick," Randy teased.

In the room, Bea was stirring when they came in. Diane helped Bea walk to the rest room while Randy stayed with Matt. Before the girls got back, there was a knock at the door. It was the detectives. "Hello again," Detective Lauer smiled. "We spoke to the desk and they said Mr. Harrington hasn't been awake much yet. Is that right?"

"Only enough to ask where he was and such," Randy answered.

"Did you tell him what you think happened with your mother?"

"No. We just told him that he had an allegoric reaction to clams. He went back to sleep before we finished the sentence. We didn't think it would be worthwhile to get him wound up."

Eastman said, "It seems his doctor thinks he came very close to dying. He said that it took a lot of clam juice to make him that sick. Although, it doesn't take much sometimes."

"He went out after two bites." Randy stated, "I never saw anyone go down that fast. He passed out in the matter of a minute."

The girls came back in the room and the detectives introduced themselves to Bea. "The nurse gave us a room we can use for your interview Miss Fedder, if you feel up to it."

"I can do that. I had a good nap this afternoon. I can't do steps or such."

"It's just down the hall," Det. Lauer smiled. "We will try to make it fast."

They left the room and Diane and Randy sat down, "Sure didn't seem to take them very long to do all their other interviews. Did it?"

"Maybe they aren't finished with them yet," Diane suggested. "Let's not borrow trouble."

Randy leaned back in the recliner and closed his eyes. He was asleep in minutes. Diane moved over to the bed and took Matt's hand. He opened his eyes, "Did you get your pills?"

"Yes, Randy gave them to me."

"Good," Matt nodded and closed his eyes again.

Then she picked up his rosary from his hand. "Would you like to recite the rosary with me?"

He nodded and started to recite it, but fell asleep after a few lines.

The interview with Bea went as expected and both detectives seemed comfortable with her answers and perspective. They told her that they had not spoken to Mrs. Berg yet and still had to talk to the grocers. Then they headed back to Matt's room.

When they entered the room, Diane was just answering the phone. "Yes, Dr. Werner?"

"She is?" Diane motioned for them to wake Randy. Matt's eyes were already open. "No, I don't believe that either Randy or I want to go see her. Do whatever you feel is necessary. At least that is my view, here. I will let you speak to Randy?"

As Diane sat down with tears rolling down her cheeks, Randy came to the phone, "This is Randy."

He listened and then responded firmly, "No. We will not. We will sign for whatever treatment you feel is necessary, but we will not see her! We told her that before and she has always managed to maneuver us back into kowtowing to her. She has gone over the line this time."

Randy shook his head and continued, "I'm sorry that she is so upset and hysterical. For what? She isn't the one on IV's or sporting a cast! What's that in the Bible about as you sow, so shall you reap? I have no sympathy for her. None. In all her ranting, has she asked how Matt is? Does she even care? Hell no! But if you think she needs sedation, do it."

Detective Lauer snapped her fingers to get Randy's attention, "Let me talk to the doctor."

Randy nodded, "Dr. Werner, Detective Lauer would like a word with you."

Lauer took the phone, "What's the problem?"

Lauer listened, nodded and then said, "We ask that if it is possible you calm her down, but don't knock her out. We need to speak with her. We're still not able to speak with Mr. Harrington. We will come back over and talk to her now, but we will have to speak to her again after we talk to some of the others. We're on our way. Oh, don't mention to her about Mr. Harrington's condition."

Detective Lauer handed Randy the phone back and said, "Seems Mrs. Berg is quite hysterical. They are going to calm her a bit, but Eastman and I are on our way over there. We'll be back in about an hour. Please, do not speak to Mr. Harrington about what is going on until we talk to him."

"We won't."

On the drive back to the hospital, Lauer looked at Eastman, "I think we should see if Mrs. Berg is concerned about Miss Fedder or Mr. Harrington."

"Are you thinking not to mention them to her? Leave it up to her?" The younger investigator asked.

Lauer nodded, "Exactly. If it was one of my kid's fiancée, I would be concerned. Wouldn't you?"

"Yes, you know Flo, I tend to believe the young folks. I think they are fine people. We have not talked to any of the staff who could more than tolerate the woman. It is just hard to believe that a fragile invalid could be so vindictive."

"Michael, don't let that tweak your heart. I have seen beautiful folks who are brutal and malicious, and big bruisers who have the kindest, most gently heart. Looks often allows bad people to get away with all sorts of things."

"I know, but I find it hard to believe and neither would a jury. I don't think they have much of a case."

"Neither do I, but I sure am going to check it out like she is a Mafia don."

Eastman laughed, "I bet you will. I do think the kid's reaction was genuine. I doubt very much they are trying to set her up."

"Me too, but maybe there is money at the bottom of it or she just pushed them to the point of no return."

Dr. Werner met the detectives at the front desk and walked back with them to her room. "She was agitated and started ringing her buzzer incessantly. Mrs. Berg doesn't handle disappointment at all well. The staff checked on her and she was working herself into a frenzied state. She was upset because her kids had not been in to see her yet."

"It didn't sound to us like there was a plan for them to see her."

"There wasn't, but that is what she wanted. I went down to see her to give her something to calm her down so she didn't have a stroke or throw herself out of the wheelchair."

"What? Does she do that?" Detective Lauer asked. "What the hell?"

"Yes, she does. She throws a major tantrum and flings herself out of bed or her chair. She has managed to bruise herself up pretty good. So far, we have managed to restrain her from breaking any bones, but mostly it was just luck. Anyway, she asked if the kids were coming to see her and I told her they were not. She hyperventilated to the point her lips turned blue. She demanded that I tell them she was so distraught so they needed to come. I shared with her than I had told them and they hoped she would be okay, but they are not coming. She flipped herself out of the chair, but she only scuffed her cheek. One of the attendants is sitting with her now until she settles down. She should be a lot better by now, but don't expect her to be calm."

"After we leave, you can knock her out. We likely won't see her again until in the morning. Oh, we found the bottle of clam juice in the trash like you expected. Glad you thought of gathering the trash for us," Eastman said.

"No problem. Well, good luck. There is a panic button in there, if she freaks out on you."

The detectives thanked Dr. Werner and then asked if it would be necessary for the attendant to stay in the room. Dr. Werner thought and then said, "I would prefer it. If you'd rather speak to her alone, I guess that's doable. May I suggest that he stays at first and if you think it is necessary, ask him to step out? Her meds might not have kicked in all the way yet."

"Sounds good," Eastman said. "Does she know we are coming?"

"None of us have told her that you are even investigating anything." Werner nodded, "She is sitting in there expecting her children to come and ask her forgiveness."

"What?" Lauer scrunched up her face.

"That's what she told me. You will have to find out for yourself what she is thinking."

"I'm looking forward to a tall, frosty pint tonight!" Lauer groaned.

They entered the room and Loretta was shocked to see two strangers there. Dr. Werner introduced her, "Loretta, two detectives from the Portland Police Department are here to ask you a few questions. Gary, you can stay with Mrs. Berg until the detectives want to talk to her alone. Then, could I ask you to stand outside the door?"

"Of course, Doctor," Gary answered. "Mrs. Berg seems to be more under control now."

The sparrow-like woman appraised the couple scathingly but snapped toward Gary, "You overgrown ape! Don't talk about me behind my back in front of me! I'm not deaf! You can get your worthless ass out of here!"

Dr. Werner put his hand on Loretta's shoulder, "Now Loretta, calm down. Gary is only here to help you. I want him to stay with you so you don't hurt yourself."

"What a load of crap! We all know you are only concerned I will file a lawsuit against this flophouse for not providing the care we pay dearly for. I had a convulsion and bruised my face. Your wretched staff should have protected me. They were totally inept in their care of me. He can stay, but tell him to keep his stupid mouth shut!"

Dr. Werner stood and introduced the couple, "This is Detectives Eastman and Lauer. They would like to ask you a few questions."

Loretta frowned at them and then snapped, "What the hell do you want? You don't look like you have the joint brain power to arrest a wino."

"We need to ask you some questions about what has been going on here," Mike Eastman knelt down near her chair.

"What do you want? I won't sue this outfit for malpractice although they deserve it. I could own this joint for all their lousy care, but I won't do that. You can have Werner drag you out of here."

"I'm going back to my office," Dr. Werner smiled at Lauer. "Contact me if you need me."

Lauer nodded and then pulled a chair up in front of Loretta Berg. Loretta glowered at her, "Don't stand on ceremony! Make yourself comfortable. With all the lard you are carrying, you no doubt can't stand very long."

Lauer gave her a crooked smile and Eastman raised his eyebrows. He wondered if this skinny woman had any idea who she was dealing with. He shook his head and thought, 'Mrs. Berg, you just hammered the first nail in your coffin'.

"No ma'am," the young man said respectfully, "We do not investigate things of that nature. We are here on two related cases. One is a case of assault and the other is a poisoning."

Loretta was taken totally by surprise, but stopped to think before she answered. She switched to the weak, pathetic voice, "I know nothing about anything like that. I am an invalid and can barely get around in my wheelchair. I spend my days stuck in this dump of a room; alone and ignored. I know nothing about anything."

"From the reports we received, you were very involved in all these events. A young lady by the name of Fedder—"

"Bea Fedder?" Loretta screeched. "That loathsome creature? That lying wretch made a charge? Against me? How ridiculous!"

"It is believed that you purposely broke her leg and thereby may have damaged her career as a dancer," Eastman continued in a steady voice.

Loretta was beginning to hyperventilate again. This was not something she had expected. She never imagined that little skank would report her to the police. Gary knelt next to her and tried to help her breath regularly. When she got control again, she slapped his hands away from her.

The more she thought about it, the madder she became. Then she started to scream, "That thing fancies herself a dancer! She did this just to blame me for her lack of talent! I couldn't be able to break anyone's leg! Look," she pointed to her own scrawny legs, "What could a tiny thing like me do to a muscle-bound Amazon like her? My word, I'm not physically capable."

"We have signed statements from both of your children and Miss Fedder that you purposely ran headlong into her legs with your wheelchair." Eastman reached out to take her hand, "We came to hear your version of events."

Loretta allowed him to take her hand and then leaned back in her chair. She considered him a minute and decided she could play this overgrown teenager like a violin. The saccharine dripped from her lips as she smiled at him, "Detective Eastman, do I look like someone who could break someone's legs? I have a new electric wheelchair and can't drive it very well."

Detective Lauer noticed the attendant Gary unintentionally snorted when she said that. She looked at him, but he quickly became stoic.

"Most days," Loretta spoke very weakly, "I can barely get out of bed or feed myself. What are you accusing me of? My goodness, young man. You seem the kind of fine, respectful son that would make your mother proud. I bet you take good care of your mother, don't you? I imagine you'd never abandon her in an institution and go running around with some half-naked dancer. Would you?"

Eastman grinned, "Ma'am, we aren't talking about me. We need your version of these events."

Loretta's demeanor had now become so fragile, long-suffering and loving one would have thought they were in the presence of a gentle deity.

"My son and daughter came to visit me after shunning me for years. They don't care if I live or die, leaving me in this squalor with barely enough help to survive. I was willing to forgive them. I am used to doing without and suffering, so they can have a good life. They waltz in here with that floozy and some defrocked priest they have been running with and begin accusing me of all sorts of things. All I ever wanted was their love. As their mother, I deserve their love after all the sacrifices I have made for them. I struggled to care for them when their worthless father walked out on us. Even though I was suffering great physical distress, I cared for them every day. Never complaining or asking for anything. They both went off to have good lives and ignored me. I was so excited to see them again. I just moved my wheelchair too fast and couldn't slow it properly."

"Did you drive into Miss Fedder?"

"Yes, I am so very weak and lost control of the wheelchair. I accidently bumped her legs. If she wasn't so clumsy, she could have move out of the way. However I was heartbroken about it, and they know it. She's worthless as a dancer, but I don't have to break her legs to destroy her career. She can do that all by herself."

"Both of your children said that it seemed you did it on purpose."

"Randy couldn't get laid for love nor money, so I imagine he'd say whatever she wanted him to say to simply get a piece. Diane is an imbecile. She hasn't had an original idea since she was born. She'd do whatever Randy said. So, what did the priest say?"

"Mr. Harrington was unable to give a report."

Lauer was watching the woman carefully. She saw a glimmer of the look the kids had mentioned. It wasn't quite a smirk, but there was a flash of glee in her countenance when Eastman said Mr. Harrington couldn't give a report. Randy had described it as the 'I just ate your cat' expression.

Silence suffocated the room. Loretta very much wanted to ask why Matt couldn't give a report and the detectives were waiting to see if she would.

Apparently she decided after a couple minutes, that they were not about to divulge any further information, so she deflected the topic, "I hope you realize that it is just an attempt for Bea to pull my son's attention to herself and away from me."

"Might be at that," Eastman nodded. "Now, as to the other charges—."

"What other charges? What else are they accusing me of? My goodness," she gave a whiny sigh, "What I must bear."

"Did you poison Matthew Harrington?"

Instantly, Loretta was livid, "Now just how do you think I could do that? The idiot choked on his sandwich or some damned thing! How could I possibly be responsible for that? I was sitting across the table from him. This is ridiculous. I can't believe that our tax dollars pay for you morons to run accusing nursing home patients of this sort of thing! I can't help it if that oaf doesn't know how to eat! Maybe you should talk to HIS mother!"

"The report says that you laced his sandwich with poison."

Mrs. Loretta Berg threw a holy fit. She shrieked and arched her back. She flung herself out of the chair and onto the floor. Gary was there to help her, but she was thrashing recklessly. Then she screeched and began to breathe erratically.

Gary looked up, "Could you push that panic button?" he pointed his head in the direction of a red knob on the wall.

Lauer pushed the button and within seconds, two more attendants rushed in. They gave Mrs. Berg a shot and lifted the tiny thing onto her bed. Dr. Werner arrived and then asked the detectives to wait in the hall.

A few minutes later, he met them there. "I have to interrupt the interview. I hope to get her blood pressure, heart rate and breathing back in safe range. I'm sorry. She will likely not be able to continue until tomorrow morning."

"She is volatile, no doubt." Detective Lauer agreed. "I think we got an idea of what she is like. Will someone be with her all night?"

"Oh yes," Werner said. "We would never leave a patient alone in this condition. If she gets much worse, we'll move her to the medical unit."

"Good, and we would appreciate it if you could make sure she is not alone, until we can talk to her again. We will be here by seven in the morning if you think she will be able to continue then."

"Yes, but if there is a change, I will call you right away."

"Thanks Doctor," Eastman shook his hand. "We appreciate all your help."

As they headed across the parking lot, Lauer shook her head, "My kids better thank God they got me for a mom instead of her."

Eastman laughed, "I'm sure they do. Did you like how she managed to bring my Mom into it?"

The middle-aged cop grinned, "I sure did. You nice, young man! I almost puked. If her kids didn't want to dump her, I would think they were nuts."

# 13

Randy made more than a few phone calls in an effort to find an attorney. He was fortunate enough to contact one who would see them that afternoon. "I will be in town, but off from Good Friday through the weekend, but I think I can have the papers to withdraw from the power of attorney ready for you. Could you and your sister come over to my office right away?"

Bea was very content to sit back in the recliner after she took another pain pill. She would keep Matt company the rest of the afternoon. Matt was beginning to cough more and seemed quite restless, but he was still rarely awake.

The nurses slowed the drip down on his IV and said he should be awake in another hour and a half.

At the attorney's office, Diane and Randy not only withdrew as her powers of attorney, but also drew up a restraining order against her, so she could no longer continue to harass them. The attorney said he would have all the paperwork ready for them to sign in the morning. After they had explained the situation with their mother, he was hired as their representative to deal with the on-going situation after they went home.

They left there and drove to the cemetery. There they sold off all their family plot, except their mother's plot and had the money from their plots transferred to pay for her final expenses and the headstone. Then they stopped at the funeral home and purchased a prepaid funeral plan for her. They would give the paperwork to their attorney in the morning. They felt they were as done with the situation as humanly possible, even though neither thought it would be that easy.

The Detectives stopped and had a very late lunch and then met with the grocers. All the statements pointed in the direction that Mrs. Berg had indeed plotted to cause Matt harm. However, legally no one could prove that she wanted to do any more than make him sick. There was little way to prove she had wanted him to die. They didn't know if the District Attorney would charge the case. Taking violent invalids off the street does not make a fine campaign poster, and the DA was running for re-election.

After their lunch, they called the hospital to check on Matt and then decided to go back to the office for an hour to give him time to wake up. They checked with the forensics lab about the trash.

The only fingerprints on the clam juice bottle belonged to the grocer delivery boy and Mrs. Berg. By checking the receipt, they were able to ascertain the clam juice was bought that morning. The grocer had only begun carrying that brand a few months before, and no other deliveries were made to the care center.

Matt's sandwich was tested and an extremely large amount of clam juice was found. The Sunrise Sandwich shop did not have clam juice in their kitchen. Nothing on their menu had clams or clam juice in it.

The detectives knocked softly on Matt's hospital room door. "Is he still sleeping?" Lauer asked.

Bea sat up and stifled a yawn, "Yes, but he has been coughing more, so I think he is more awake. Come in."

Detective Eastman smiled and helped Bea to her feet. "How is the leg?"

The three went to the side of the bed and Bea touched his shoulder, "Matt, there are some people here that need to speak to you. Can you talk to them?"

Matt blinked and opened his eyes, "Is your leg better? Oh, hello."

"We're sorry to bother you, but I'm Detective Lauer and this is my partner, Detective Eastman. You are Matt Harrington?"

Puzzled and dopey, Matt nodded, "This is Bea. She has a cast."

"We've met. We would like to ask you some questions. Would that be okay?"

Matt looked at Bea and she said, "Matt, it will be okay. I'm going to the restroom and I'll be right back."

"Diane?" he asked.

"She's at a meeting with Randy. They will be back soon. Would you like your bed up a bit?"

"Please."

Bea raised the bed and then left the room. Matt ran his free hand through his hair and gave them a sheepish grin. "I have a cough. Bea said I caught it from the clams."

"We heard about that," Lauer chuckled. "We need to talk to you about Loretta Berg."

"Oh, she's not nice at all! She drove her wheelchair right smack into Bea and broke her leg! Just like a bumper car! Smash bang! I never saw the likes of it! You need to stand behind the sofa. Be careful when you're around her," he yawned.

Lauer and Eastman shared a smile over his groggy reply. Then Eastman asked, "Do you think she did it on purpose?"

"Of course! Aimed right at her like an arrow! Full speed ahead! Moves pretty fast for an old gal."

"Really?"

"Yup. Smack dab into her legs."

Eastman asked, "Isn't she too feeble?"

"They need to take her motor away! She's dangerous."

"I doubt she could be dangerous. She is too feeble," Eastman said.

"Don't kid yourself!" Matt warned the young detective, "And hey, don't let her near your privates! She'll have you singing soprano in a heartbeat! I almost passed out!"

Then he collapsed into a fit of coughing. The two detectives looked at each other wondering if they should call the nurse, but he began to start breathing more regularly. Then he held his chest and they put the light on.

The nurse came in, "What's up?"

"He was coughing very hard and then grabbed his chest."

Matt looked at the nurse with tears in his eyes, "It hurts to cough."

"I know," she said. "Do you feel any numbness?"

"No numbs. Just my ribs."

"They are complaining because you've given them quite a work out. Maybe you should try to sleep again."

"Okay," Matt said hoarsely, as he slid back in his bed.

The nurse turned to the couple, "Try to keep your visit short. Okay?"

"Yes," Lauer said. "We will be leaving in a minute."

After the nurse left the room, Lauer said, "Mr. Harrington, as best as you know, did Mrs. Berg intentionally try to hurt Bea Fedder."

"She sure did."

"Did you mention to her that you were allergic to clams?"

"Ah," he thought a minute, "Yes. She said I was a picky eater about the chowder, so I told her. Is she allergic, too?"

"No, I don't believe so."

"Oh."

"Did she try to hurt you?"

"Yup, that little thing brought us to our knees in a day! She said she would, too!" Then he whispered, "She's meaner than hell and doesn't like anybody."

Then he started coughing like crazy again. Detective Lauer helped him get situated in his bed again while Eastman went to help Bea back in to the room. Then they bid their goodbyes.

In the car, Lauer said, "He didn't say much, but I think he was honest. I don't think he was in any condition to be lying."

Eastman smiled, "No, I think he told us the truth. The statement would never stand up, but we will type it up and he can look it over before he signs it. He was kinda funny."

"Wonder what all he was on?" Lauer laughed. "You know, he is right. Mrs. Berg is very effective."

It was almost five o'clock when Diane and Randy returned to the hospital. Bea was sleeping again and Matt was coughing, but much more awake.

"I'm getting rather hungry," Randy said. "I think I will take the girls down to the cafeteria, if you don't mind, Matt?"

"No, I think I will take a nap. I have never been so tired. Did I dream that some people came to ask questions?"

"No, they really did. They were detectives."

"What did they want to talk to me about?" Matt was still vague on what the day had been.

"Matt." Randy sat on the edge of the bed, "They came to talk to you about what Mom did to Bea and you."

Matt frowned and was trying to concentrate for a bit. "I sort of remember them asking about Bea's leg. Yah, I remember that. They asked what Mrs. Berg did at the restaurant."

"No one told them that. You must have." Randy said.

"I thought they knew. They asked me if Loretta had tried to hurt me."

"They were referring to what she did to your sandwich," Diane said. "Matt, she put clam juice on it to try to kill you."

Matt's eyes opened broadly and his mind tried desperately to grasp what they were saying. Finally, he said, "I don't eat clams. You mean, she fed them to me on purpose? She knew they made me sick."

"Yes," Randy patted he shoulder, "She did it on purpose. She tried to get rid of both you and Bea, any way she could. She tried to kill you."

Matt frowned, "I never had anyone try to kill me before. I have to tell Ian."

"After we have dinner, do you want to call him?"

"No, I need to take my nap. I'm so tired. I feel drunk," Matt pulled his pillow. "Someone tried to kill me. Go figure."

The trio returned to Matt's room to find him having coffee with a Catholic priest who did visitation on patients. "I told the nurse I was going through coffee withdrawal, so she gave in. I've hung around Elton too long and can't make it a full day without coffee. They even brought me some cream of wheat stuff. Really yukky, but it filled me up. I feel better than I have in hours!"

They were talking about the upcoming Easter masses. The middle-aged priest introduced himself to the others, "I'm Father Sebastian. I have been visiting with Matt. He has told me a little about your adventurous visit here."

Randy shook his hand and then introduced the ladies, "I'm Randy, this is my sister Diane and my fiancée Bea."

"You must be the ballerina."

The group talked for an hour, and told Father Sebastian the whole sordid story. Then Randy said, "Tomorrow is going to be awful. The detectives are going to finish their investigation and then talk to the

District Attorney. Then we will know if they are going to charge Mom or not. In the morning, Diane and I are signing the papers so we are legally out of her life. Our attorney is going over to talk to her and break the news to her. She will be livid."

The priest listened intently and then asked, "Don't you think that she will be depressed that she lost the last of her family?"

Diane responded, "Won't matter that she lost her family; she will be furious because she lost control. She always beats us to death with how much she loves us, but the next sentence is how awful we are and what she wants us to do for her."

"I think she honestly would feel as bad about losing us—as a cat would feel if someone took an injured mouse away! There would be no one left to torment," Randy said coldly.

"Does your mom go to Mass at Shorepoint? I go there frequently, but I don't remember having met her. However, that doesn't mean that she wasn't there. I may have just forgotten."

"I don't know," Diane said. "I doubt it though. She never makes any mention of it. To hear her tell it, she is stuck in a dungeon and left to eat gruel with her fingers."

Sebastian chuckled, "Shorepoint would be a dungeon I wouldn't mind being in! I am in and out of many retirement homes, and that is the nicest one I have ever seen. If you don't mind, I may go over there and visit with her tonight. I think I'd like to prepare her for tomorrow. Then she wouldn't be blindsided by the restraining order and all that. It could be very difficult to find out you are all alone; even if you worked diligently all your life to bring about that outcome."

Matt listened carefully and then said, "I think it would be a good idea guys. No matter how we feel about her, she is still one of God's children and we need to show compassion."

Randy squinted at Matt, "I suppose you think we should go crawling back to her."

"Not at all. But if Father Sebastian wants to help her, it could be beneficial to all of us. You told me that she still is your mom. I know you still care about her. Neither of you guys are going to walk away and not even care about it. I know you better than that. You both spent time today arranging things so she would have care and a decent funeral, when the time comes. I don't think that you should have anything to do with her. I am in complete agreement about that."

Bea nodded, "I agree. Just because she is so horrible, doesn't give us the option to be as bad. We shouldn't be around her, and I think if she ends up in jail that would be fine, but we have no need to be cruel. I don't want to go six months down the road and have you feel terrible because you did this. I want us to walk away knowing you were firm but did everything you could to help her."

Randy groaned, "She destroyed our Dad, hurt you guys and made our lives hell! I want her to pay for that. I just want to strangle her!"

Father Sebastian put his arm on his shoulder, "I understand. I'm impressed that you didn't do it years ago. I don't vaguely suggest you continue a personal relationship with her. I think it is not only dangerous and foolish; it only continues the behavior. From what you've said, no matter how limited, every time you even talk to her on the phone; she thinks that she has 'her mouse to taunt'. She doesn't seem to understand threats or that everyone has their limits. But as demonically as she behaves, she is still a human being."

"Borderline," Randy grunted. "I guess you're right. What can it hurt to have her talk to a priest? No skin off my nose. It just makes me so angry that now it seems like Diane and I are the bad guys and she is sitting like a queen."

"Well, if you give me permission, I will talk to her and point out to her that your behavior is not unexpected and that she is entitled to suffer for what she did. I won't allow her to blame everyone else. I'll try to make her appreciate that this is of her own making. Agree?"

Everyone nodded in agreement, and Randy said, "I guess you're right. I'm just so damned mad at her."

"I will make you a promise," Father Sebastian said, "She will understand before I leave that this is her fault and no one else's doing. Deal?

"I'd like that."

"So Matt, when are you checking out of here?"

"Doc said tomorrow late morning. Then we have to see what is going on here when we can leave town."

Randy said, "We won't leave until we hear from the detectives what is going to happen. So I think we will still be here Friday."

"I know you folks are really busy, but if you can find time, come see us on Good Friday, St. Ignatius. Okay?"

"We'll do that, if we can," Bea answered. "Will we see you again?"

"Here is my phone number and I need yours. I will make it a point to let you know how things are going with your Mom if you would like."

Randy wrote down their phone numbers, "Yes, I would really like that. Thanks, Father."

After a word of prayer, he left the room. It was quiet for a bit and then Randy said, "I bet he thinks I'm a real jerk."

"No, I don't think he does, Randy." Matt said. "He is in the soul business. You know clergy will walk with anyone on the way to the gallows to offer spiritual comfort. That doesn't mean they want to play ping pong with them!"

"Yea gads, how long were you without oxygen? Ping pong?" Randy laughed.

"You know what I mean. I think he appreciates your situation. Don't worry about it. But admit it, it will be kinda nice to have someone that can keep us informed what she's up to."

"That's no lie," Randy chuckled, "Bea and I are going to look around the grounds, if you guys would like to have some time together. Then I think we need to get some sleep. Or do you want someone to stay with you here tonight?"

"Not necessary. I feel pretty good. Thanks. I think you guys need the rest more than I do now. I slept almost all day."

Bea and Randy left them room and Diane took Matt's hand, "What a day!"

"You can say that again!"

"Do you want to call your folks and Schroeders?"

"Yes, I should do that. What time is it in North Dakota? I would like to talk to them before they go milking."

"Yes, and then you have to talk to your Mom. She was flipping out!" Diane giggled.

Nora answered the phone and started to cry when she heard Matt's voice, "I was so worried about you! How are you? And how is Bea?"

"I can go home tomorrow. The doctors just want to make sure I got all of the toxins out of my system. My lungs were paralyzed or something. My cough is a lot better and I am more awake now. I finally got some coffee! I was so groggy from the stuff that counteracted the toxins, I was like a tired drunk!"

"You still sound very hoarse. How is Bea?"

"She has to have her cast on for three months. It'll be a major setback for her career. But you know Bea. She is always so positive and can be happy about anything. She is a good egg. I will let Diane explain the other stuff to you. I only learned a bit ago that I didn't eat the clam juice by accident. How is Grandpa? Is he missing our rides in his old Ford?"

"Darrell stopped by and gave him a ride yesterday. When he came in, he said Grandpa was giving him instructions the whole way. Even directions on how to put the key in the ignition! You know how Grandpa Lloyd can be!" Nora giggled.

"Glad to hear that. At least I won't be the only 'dumb one' in the clan."

Nora laughed, "Maybe not, but you still rank near the top!"

"Here I thought I loved you."

"I hope it isn't too much of a disappointment. Oh, there is a little girl here who has been down in the dumps since she heard that you were in the hospital! Can I go get her so she can speak to you?"

"I'd like that. Are the boys around?" Matt asked.

"Here is CJ. He is getting ready to go do Chicken Chores."

The little seven-year-old excitedly took the phone, "Hi. I'm so glad you aren't dead!"

Matt laughed, "I'm rather glad, too. Nora said you are going to take care of the chickens?"

"Yah, the baby chicks don't have their feathers yet. Maybe they will when you get home. How soon will you be home? Tomorrow?"

"No, on Monday if all goes well."

"Mr. Matt, Clarence is bouncing on his one and the other foot to talk to you. Do you want to tell him hi?"

"That would be good. Have a good day, CJ. It was great talking to you."

Then the eight-year-old Clarence got on the line, "You all better now?"

"Just about. I get out of the hospital tomorrow. What's going on with you?"

"Well, Mr. Darrell and I gave Grandpa a ride and then polished up the old Ford like you do. We did chores, and I finally earned my second goat! Now I have Hansel and Gretel! We've been playing with Skipper and taking care of Lucky and Murphy. Murphy started hiding behind the dryer."

"Yah, he did that once in a while when I was home. Guess he thinks it is warm there."

"That's what Mr. Darrell said. Can I ask you something?"

"Of course, what is it?"

"Will you be home in time to teach me for that barn dance thing?"

"I will do that. And I'm pretty certain Nora will, too."

"Does she know how?"

"She and Mister are both great dancers! Just ask either of them and they will be able to help."

"Okay, get well! I have to hand the phone to Clarissa. She is acting like she is going to have a cow!"

Matt heard Clarissa yell at him and then take the phone, "Don't listen to him. Okay?"

"How's my girl?"

"You remembered! I was so worried we'd have to put you in the ground, but Missus said you were getting better. Are you? Because I don't like putting everybody I know in the ground."

"I don't either, Clarissa. I'm okay and will be home soon. Diane is taking good care of me."

"Can I ask her a mostest important question?" the little girl asked.

"Of course, here she is. Love you, Clarissa."

"Me, too."

Diane took the phone, "Hello, Clarissa."

Clarissa giggled and then lowered her voice so it was almost inaudible, "Did you find our dresses yet? I don't want Mister to hear."

"I haven't had time yet because I've been busy with Matt. I will go tomorrow. How does that sound?"

"Good. Do you need to ask Missus what my fit size is?"

"I know it already, Clarissa. Don't worry. It will be wonderful, pink and soft."

Clarissa giggled, "I love you. Mister is here now, so I think you should talk to him. Bye bye. Give Mr. Matt the mostest biggest hug in the whole wide world."

"I will," Diane said, "I'm handing the phone over to Matt."

Matt and Elton had a long talk and discussed the situation. After about ten minutes, Matt was coughing a lot again, so they decided to hang up. Then they called Matt's grandparent's home in Boston. A babysitter answered and said they had all gone out for dinner, but she could get them if it was an emergency. Matt told her to just say that he called, was doing much better and that he would call in the morning.

The priest checked at the front desk for Mrs. Berg's room. Then he went down the hall and knocked. After a short time, Mrs. Berg wheeled her chair to the door to answer it. When she saw a priest, she scowled, "What do you want? Haven't you squeezed enough money out of your pitiful congregation that now you have to go door to door in an old people's home?"

"I'm not here for a donation. I came to speak with you. I learned today that you will be receiving some news tomorrow and thought you might like an opportunity to talk about it before it happens," Father Sebastian said calmly. "May I come in? I am Father Sebastian from Saint Ignatius."

She swung the door open and wheeled herself back to the table, "Suit yourself. It better be good. I'm expecting my children."

"That is what I am here about."

"What the hell would you know about my brats?"

"I met with them this afternoon. Randy told me that their attorney is coming over to see you tomorrow morning. I felt it would be wise to let you know beforehand so you had time to prepare yourself."

"Why don't they come themselves? Did they go sniveling to you? I suppose that defrocked priest died and now they are bawling all over the place."

"This is something, apparently they have felt they needed to do for some time, but these last few days it became apparent they had to do it now," the priest stood in front of Mrs. Berg. "May I sit down?"

"Just don't get comfortable," the withered woman snarled. "So, what is it that the wimps couldn't tell me to my face?"

"They have made arrangements so they will no longer have your power of attorney. They have named a trust officer to be in charge of paying for your care from your funds."

Her eyes flashed and she smirked, "And you heard about my money and wanted to get your mitts on it!"

"No, Ma'am. That is in the hands of a trust officer. Your children paid for your funeral plot . . . ."

"We had a family plot already. You're lying."

"No, you did. They sold their plots and assigned the money for your headstone and committal when the time comes."

"That's moronic. Just where in the hell are they going to be planted except in the family plot? What gives you the right to come in here and tell me all this crap?"

"Randy will share a family plot with Bea and Diane has a space near the infant son that has already passed on. They do not want to be buried here."

"Ungrateful asses! Let them go buy some big fancy place! See if I care. What the hell good are they going to do me when they are dead anyway! They don't pay attention to me now! All they do is accuse me of horrible things. Anyone can just take one look and know I am just a weak invalid. All I have ever wanted is my children's love!" Then she started to weep.

The priest patted her shoulder and she sprang back, "Keep your hands off me! Why are you doing this to me? I have been nothing but good. You should go talk to them! They are the ones running around with trash and ignoring their responsibilities to their mother. You know it says in the commandments, honor you father and mother."

"It does, but it doesn't say that you have to live with them all your life and care for their every whim. They do honor you, even today after all that has transpired."

"They never did. They'll be back! They will be crawling back to me as soon as the realize they can't live on their own! They are worthless, stupid, soporific blood-suckers. I have never needed them; they need me! They'll be back. You wait! They will be calling me and asking for my advice."

"No, they won't."

"Well, then I'll call them."

"Loretta, they have filed a restraining order against you. You are to make no contact with them."

That is the first time the priest saw fear in her eye. She studied him for a minute and then said seriously, "No. You're lying. Get out of here! I will push my buzzer and they will take you out. What did you talk my kids into doing? Why is everyone being so cruel to me?"

"Loretta, I will go if you truly want me to, or we can talk. Do you have someone else you would like to talk to?"

"Hell no. There is no one! They all walked out on me! Every cretin in the bunch."

"I imagine many of them didn't like all the names you call them. Do you think that might be some it?"

"It isn't my fault they are all stupid."

The priest smiled, "I know it is difficult sometimes to talk to people who drive you crazy; but we should try to remember they probably cannot help it. We should try to be as kind as we can to them."

"You just do that! I don't have time."

"What else do you have to do?"

'What's that supposed to mean?"

"It was simply a question."

She banged the table with her fist, "I hate this. As soon as I can get out of here, I'm moving away. They can go rot. I will get a nice place and some decent help. They will be sorry."

"You may have that opportunity. My understanding is that you have to move from Shorepoint. I think that you were warned before and were told the other day that you have to find different accommodations."

"They are just saying that because they want more money."

The priest was not swayed, "No, they don't want you here any longer. I believe you have three weeks to find another place. It seems that you have been a troublemaker and unnecessarily mean to the staff. They can't put up with that. Have you had any thoughts about where you will go?"

"I'm going to get the kids to buy a house and they can take care of me. After all, I am their mother. Now they are abandoning me, just like their no good father. I can't find a place while I am stuck in this dump." She looked at the priest pleadingly, "What am I to do? I think they just want my money."

"Not at all. They want nothing to do with it. You have a tidy sum and it should care for you for a few years if you are careful. They have not spend one cent on themselves."

"You sure seem to know a lot about it, for someone that doesn't want it."

"I have no need for your money and I think that you will need it. I hear the police are investigating some things you are involved in, so you may have to hire a good attorney."

"That's ridiculous. No one will charge me with anything. I'm a little, old lady in a wheel chair and weak as a pin. I have no problems there." The lady smirked to herself, "Don't get your tunic in a panic, sonny. I have this all under control. Shorepoint isn't about to toss me out. I'm a good payer. My kids will come crawling back. Don't worry yourself a bit. Just watch me and I will show you how it's done!"

"Mrs. Berg, do you realize that you have pushed everything too far? You really have. You have put yourself into a corner and it will be extremely difficult to emerge unscathed."

"You just watch and learn. I got your phone number on this little card, if I need you I will call. You just run along," the woman tapped the card with the priest's phone number on the table.

"Would you like a prayer before I go?"

"I'd like you to get the hell out of my face! I want to watch my television program. I don't need you or your hocus pocus."

"Okay, but if you change your mind, you can call me anytime. Someone will get in touch with me right away. I would be more than willing to help."

"Yah, yah," she snarled. "Don't let the door crack you in the ass on the way out."

"Good night, Mrs. Berg. I will stop back tomorrow."

"Don't waste your energy."

Matt was rather wound up and found it difficult to sleep, even though he was tired. He had to admit, he was very sorry he had missed talking to his Mom. He smiled to himself when he acknowledged that no matter how old you get, it is still nice to talk to your mom. He felt badly for Diane and Randy. They hadn't had that since they were little kids. He wondered how Loretta was as a young mother, before the meningitis. It is hard to imagine that she was kind and loving then. He guessed it was correct that we all had the capability to be really horrible inside us. It seemed to depend on which part of us we wished to foster. Although, he doubted Loretta had imagined this turnout.

He worried for Diane and Randy. They wanted so much to have normal lives, but neither had found being a part of a normal life easy. Diane was forever withdrawing and getting suspicious. She severely lacked self-confidence. While Randy seemed very self-confident, he usually managed to not get involved. One didn't have to know him very long to realize how fragile that confidence really was.

Now they were both settling into marriages and in-law families that were large and loving. While they seemed to appreciate it, Matt knew it would not be an easy thing to do. Diane had a terrible time accepting love for what it was. Mrs. Berg had instilled mistrust and doubt into her children very well. Matt himself had only dealt with her on the phone and she had him ready to jump off a cliff.

Matt also knew that neither of her kids could just walk away from her without having someone to keep them notified about what was going on with her. The responsibility that Loretta had instilled with in them would fade in time, but not that easily. Realistically, not knowing what someone like her was up to, was downright frightening. The young people all were rather certain that while she was weak, she was a lot more capable of getting around than she portrayed. None of them would be surprised to find her walking, though maybe just a shuffle, into the room at any time.

He was glad they could keep in contact with Sebastian, so he could let them know simply how she was doing, where she was and so on. He had been a priest long enough to know that one shouldn't turn their back completely on anyone. Everyone was a soul that needed salvation, even though not everyone could help that person, someone should. He felt that Sebastian also realized that the kids would have a much more difficult time just shutting her out than they imagined. Father Sebastian could bridge that gap for them, and Matt knew he would.

Matt was looking forward to that first appointment with Dr. Samuels when they got back to Bismarck. Both Samuels and Matt had underestimated this little woman. They knew she was devious and cruel, but little did either imagine the extent of it.

Matt leaned back in his hospital bed and tried to get comfortable. It was difficult to accept that someone actually, truly and actively had wanted to kill him. As the detectives had told the others, it might have been she only wanted to make him sick but they all knew without a doubt, she wanted him dead. Matt was not so naive to think that everyone loved him, but he honestly never thought anyone would want to kill him, literally. It was a weird, unpleasant feeling, to know that you were that hated.

He wondered how often Diane and Randy had felt that way. It made him shudder. Then he remembered that Diane told him sometime in his foggy sleep, that she was planning their wedding. He had waited so long for her to say that. He hadn't thought he might have to die before she would do it.

Their relationship had certainly not been a cakewalk, but this was over the top. He loved her, but had to admit that he was still worried. He knew he couldn't take it on their roller coaster much longer, before he had to get off. He didn't want to, but his tolerance level had dipped very low. There had to be fine people out there who carried less baggage. Less than a week before, Diane could barely speak to him in a civil tone, for no reason except her internal doubts. He guessed he had developed a high degree of mistrust himself.

He knew Bea had. She was a wonderful person, forgiving and kind. She loved Randy, but she also loved her career in the ballet, and she was very talented. The couple had decided that after they married, they would leave New York. Then Bea would teach dance so she could be married and have a family. She would give up her career, but not her dance. Now it was questionable she would even be able to do that. While they all put a fine light on her getting back to the ballet company, they all knew that it was iffy. Three months of cast and then slow recovery would set her back a long ways. Loretta did an excellent job on destroying Bea's dream. No matter that she didn't blame Randy for his mother's actions, but Bea would still always know it was his mom that did it. It would be there between them and neither could change it.

# 14

As the sun was coming up, Detective Lauer came into the station carrying her coffee mug. She trundled over to her messy desk and pushed some papers aside to find a flat place to put her mug. "Your old lady must have kicked you out of bed early this morning."

Mike Eastman laughed, "She did. What's your excuse?"

"Couldn't sleep worth a darn," the middle-aged lady sat down and set her purse on the floor. "This case is really bugging me. I know Berg did it, on purpose. I figure if she gets away with it; she'll only try again. I have no doubt about that. Can it be proven? Probably not. Even if we could talk the DA into even charging the case; she'd likely walk. I don't know how to proceed. I think that at the very least, we need to throw the fear of God into the old bag. Maybe it would slow her down before she tried again. I'm convinced she will."

"I was thinking that, too. I mean, this was totally premeditated, without an ounce of remorse and she put a lot of energy into it. She wants her kids to take her out of Shorepoint and take care of her. Period. Like Diane said, she wasn't happy before when it was like that. I doubt if it would make her happy now. She doesn't want to be happy. I know folks that would give their eyeteeth to be in her position. She is in the best place in the state. Shorepoint not only has great care, good food and all that; it has great social activities for anyone who wants to participate. She should be in some of those rat-infested scrapheaps some folks have to live in . . . and they are nice people!"

"You notice, she has never asked about Harrington?"

"She referred to him as being dead, once. I think she thinks he is. Why would she ask? She had every intention of killing him and certainly isn't mourning. If it had been done as a prank, she would be beside herself. She certainly isn't very sympathetic toward Bea! Good grief, she can't say a decent word about her! She is a great gal. She is pretty, dainty and graceful, not to mention a hell of a lot nicer than most folks. This skinny old witch talks about her like she is a deformed bonehead."

"Wow! Wouldn't want to be that . . . . a deformed bonehead!" Lauer giggled.

Mike shook his head, "Drink your coffee."

"So, how do you think we should proceed?"

Mike leaned back in his squeaky chair, "This really needs grease."

"You say that every time you sit in it. It has been four years and you still haven't oiled it."

"I know. I only say it needs it. I never said I would do it," he chuckled.

"How many days do I have until retirement?" Flo pretended to look at the calendar.

"You will miss me when you do." Mike answered. "I was wondering if we should give her a taste of it. I mean, bring her down her for interrogation. Let her sit in that gray, bare room to be questioned, without an attendant. Somewhere that she's not in charge."

"I'm itching to do that, but I don't know if we can justify dragging her down here yet. How about we question her without an attendant and get her wound up? Then we can leave and give her some time to simmer before we bring her down. We could probably get some word back from the DA by then so we know if we just need to scare her or actually arrest her."

"Sounds like a good idea. Let's go, Flo Baby!" Mike teased. "After we wind her up, I will spring for a big breakfast! I always say there is nothing like freaking out a bad guy to work up an appetite!"

Flo smiled, "Boy did I get the pick of the litter when they drug you in here!"

"Yah, aren't you the lucky one!"

They knocked at Mrs. Berg's door and she snarled, "About time you lazy asses brought my morning slop."

The detectives were shocked when they saw Loretta Berg. While she had been neat as a pin, dressed to the nines and layered with makeup the day before; this morning her hair was straggled. It hung like unraveled rope. She wore no makeup and a cotton housecoat over a cotton nightgown. She looked very elderly version of herself. The woman glared at them, "What the hell are you doing here?"

"We were unable to finish getting your statement yesterday. We'd like to finish this up."

"Come back later," Mrs. Berg snapped and swung the door closed. "I haven't had my breakfast yet."

Detective Eastman smiled and braced the door open with his foot, "You don't seem to understand, Mrs. Berg. This is not a request. If you don't talk to us here, we will take you downtown and question you there!"

"Downtown? Are you kidding me? You guys will never do that to a poor, fragile lady like me."

Lauer entered the room, "Look here, Berg. The United States doesn't have royalty. You are just like everyone else!"

Loretta Berg's eyes flew open and she backed up. That thought apparently had never entered her head before. It was only momentary phase and she regained her stance rapidly, "I will have to call for an attendant."

Lauer said forcefully, "No. We will call if it needs be, but we are just going to visit. There is nothing we need to talk about you might get physically upset about, unless you are hiding something. As you said, a sweet little thing like you would never have nasty secrets," Lauer glared at her.

Mrs. Berg didn't like this turn of events at all. She moved her chair toward the table and motioned for them to sit down. Mrs. Berg read people rather well and was certain that this Lauer woman was no pushover. She turned her attention to the younger detective. 'Yes,' she thought. 'He is still wet behind the ears. I can handle him. Keep calm, Loretta and you will get this nonsense behind you.'

On the way over, the detectives had decided that Detective Eastman should take the lead with the questioning because he had a bit of a rapport with her. Lauer set up her notebook on the table and readied herself to take notes.

"Okay, we were just discussing Mr. Harrington's poisoning," Eastman began.

"Why do you keep saying poison? He choked. Big damned deal."

"No, the lab reported he was poisoned."

Mrs. Berg looked puzzled and tried to read the expression on the faces of the detectives, "Like arsenic or cyanide? I never had anything do to with anything like that! I don't know who would do that!"

"No, those aren't the only two poisons in the world." Eastman wasn't smiling and looked right into her eyes, "You don't seem very upset about what happened to your daughter's fiancée."

"Why would I? He seemed like a nosy meddler who never stuck to anything in his life. He was probably a charlatan and just was after Diane for her money. She is such a worthless twit she probably figured she can't do any better. It is the best thing that ever happened to her that is he out of the picture."

"Really? You seem to feel very strongly about it. Did you feel motivated to help get him out of the picture? It sounds like it."

"What? I never said anything like that. You asked me why I didn't feel bad about him. Should I have lied? Hell no. I don't care about that skank Bea either. She is just looking for a sugar daddy. You wouldn't want your children to be taken advantage of, would you?"

"Did they think they were being taken advantage of by them? They seemed rather happy."

"They are too dumb to figure it out. A mother has to take care of things for her children."

"Mrs. Berg, could you tell us what interaction you had with Mr. Harrington. Start from when you met."

"He came in, then everyone fussed over the clumsy dancer's legs and then they left. He did take my chair into the Angus Room that night, and was very nice to me."

"I understand you had a private interaction with him that evening, while the others were at the buffet?"

Mrs. Berg snapped, "Who the hell told you that? It was nothing. He made a pass at me and I told him it was inappropriate. After all, he was engaged to my daughter! He told me he would make me pay for rejecting him. Later he told Randy something and got him all bent out of shape. Randy took me home before I got to finish my dinner. It was all Matt's fault, not mine! I am the victim of his unwelcome advances! You don't see me whining to everyone."

"No, you haven't. I will give you that," Lauer agreed.

Mrs. Berg gave her a dirty look and then turned back to Eastman. "So that is why you think I fed him arsenic? My goodness, you people don't have enough to keep you occupied."

"Could you tell us what you did yesterday morning, from the time you got up?"

Mrs. Berg made a face, "How detailed do I need to get? Want to know if how I put my undies on or what?"

Detective Lauer looked at her, "Actually, I am curious about that. I understand you usually require assistance getting dressed. Yet yesterday, you did it yourself. How did that happen?"

"I do it whenever I can. I try very hard to be as independent as possible, even though I have great physical challenges. I have to work at it. I hate being a burden on everyone," Loretta Berg said so softly it was almost impossible to hear her.

"I got up and worked on my crossword puzzle. Then I went down to the consulting room so no one would have to come get me. I was so anxious to see my family again. I could hardly wait to see them."

"Did you make any phone calls or see anyone in the morning."

Loretta's eyes flashed, "Why?"

"It is a simple question. Did or did you not talk to or see anyone in the morning before the meeting."

She stared a minute, thinking very hard. Then she answered, "I called the grocer and had them deliver some things for Bloody Marys. I thought that when the kids were done with the meeting, they might want to join me for a toddy. You know, they are going to buy a house and take me to live with them."

Lauer shook her head, "Not from what we've heard. We hear they are severing all ties with you."

"That is an ugly rumor this priest from St. Ignatius started because he wants to get control of my money. You know how they are. They can't wait to get your money into the Vatican's coffers."

Lauer wrinkled her brow, "Really? I wasn't aware of all that."

"You should be looking into that instead of annoying a little, old lady."

"I understand that you are only fifty-nine years old. That isn't elderly by a long shot," Eastman pointed out.

"Years maybe, but physically, I'm as feeble as a ninety-year-old."

Eastman even raised his eyebrows at that. "So, what did you order from the store?"

"I can't remember, sonny. Tomato juice, vodka and oh, some perfume. Mine was all gone and I had none."

Lauer looked over to her dresser. On top were several bottles of perfume on a mirrored tray, "Looks like you have several bottles there."

Mrs. Berg spun her head to look and said, "Ah, they are for show. Is it illegal to buy perfume?"

"Not at all," Eastman said. "But it is to lie to the police during an investigation."

"You can't do anything to me. No one will believe I did anything wrong."

"Think carefully, did you speak to anyone else before the meeting?"

Loretta thought, "I guess Marie from the front desk and the delivery guy from the sandwich shop. They were there when I went into the consulting room. Marie unlocked the door for us."

"How long were you there alone with the sandwiches?"

"Only a second or so. The others came in to the meeting right after they left. I remember thinking the sandwich shop had cut it close. I couldn't have been alone for more than a second."

"It is our understanding that you were there alone over ten minutes. More than enough time to put poison in Mr. Harrington's sandwich."

"Oh my word, how on earth would I even know which one was his?"

"Marie told you when she took your order."

"Oh, I guess she told me what everyone ordered. Now I suppose you think I put clam juice on everyone's sandwich."

Lauer turned and snapped, "How did you know he was poisoned with clam juice?"

"You told me that."

"No, we never mentioned it."

"Well, someone did."

"No one did. The only way you would know is because you put it in his sandwich."

Loretta started to hyperventilate and Lauer pushed the panic button. The attendants came in and the detectives left.

In the car, the two detectives looked at each other. "That old bat is as guilty as sin. I'm sure glad she isn't my mother. She is awful," Mike said.

"What's with that whiny-nicey stuff she pulls? She makes my skin crawl." Lauer put her notebook in her purse, "Where are you taking me for this fancy breakfast?"

"I never said fancy, I said big. I think Husky's Truck Stop."

"Sounds good to me!"

Matt was awake early. The lab tech came in to take his blood. "You are certainly taking enough blood there!"

The lab tech chuckled, "Yes, I raise roses and you know how they like blood. It is high in iron."

"Hm. Nice to know I'm making the sacrifice for a good cause!"

"No, they want to check to make sure you are rid of all your toxins, and then we can spring you from this joint. You might make it out of here in time to see the Easter bunny."

"I hope. Tomorrow is Good Friday. Wow, this week went fast." Matt mumbled to himself, "I guess having someone try to murder you can do that."

"I'll take your word for it." The tech grinned, "Next time, I would suggest you take your vacation where people like you!"

Matt laughed, "Good idea!"

The aide brought in his breakfast tray. He was delighted since he was starving. There was real food on it! He had ham, scrambled eggs and three pancakes. There was orange juice and bless them, a little pot of coffee! After he relished every morsel of his breakfast, he decided to call his family.

He dialed his Grandparents home and waited for the answer. He knew that Nana and Pappy were always up by five. Nana answered, "Oh my little Mattie, how is my boy?"

"I'm good Nana. I feel much better and I think I'll get out of the hospital today. I won't know for sure until the doctor comes by, but I think so."

"I must thank the good Lord. My word, this family has no shortage of cops and the one who isn't, almost gets murdered. It just goes to show you."

Matt chuckled, "Shows you what, Nana?"

She giggled, "That we must never leave you alone. You attract trouble like a magnet! I'm so glad you are on the mend. Your Mom is here. I imagine I'd better let her talk to you."

"Thanks Nana. I love you."

Mo grabbed the phone, "How is my boy? Are you okay? Do you need me to come down there? I can leave right away! I just knew I should have gone yesterday, but Coot wouldn't let me."

"It is okay Mom. I'm doing much better. I just wanted to talk to you and tell you how much I love you."

She started to cry, "Now why did you go and do that? You made me weep! I love you too, Laddie. I was so worried."

"I thought you might be. But I had great hospital care and everyone has been great to me."

"Not everyone! Did they throw that old wench in the slammer? She should be locked in the tower until the Lord comes on Judgment Day! If I ever get my hands on her . . ."

"Mom. It is okay. She is really a piece of work, but she is a pathetic miserable creature. She needs our prayers."

"I'll give her my prayers all right! Lord Above, Mattie! There was almost a posse of irate Harrington menfolk heading down that way. And North Dakota? My land sakes, the Englemann clan was fitting a fighting unit that would rival D-Day! The priests Vicaro and Fedder signed on as generals. Good thing for that old bag of bones that calmer heads like mine prevailed."

"Yes, Mom," Matt laughed. "I'm glad you were calm."

"Look, nobody gets to poison my kids but me!" she blustered. "No, I don't think that is what I meant."

"You have always leaned toward a good whack, Mom. Poison isn't your weapon of choice. You know, we really had no idea what Diane and Randy were dealing with. I don't know how they came out as sane as they did."

"How are they doing? Is Diane okay? And Bea, how is she?"

"They are good and seem resolved to sever all ties with Loretta. I think it would be the best for everyone. We met a priest here, Father Sebastian, who volunteered to keep an eye on her and let them know how she is doing. But they will no longer have anything to do with her. Bea is good. I know she feels terrible about her dancing, but she is making the best of it. She will be in a cast for at least three months."

"Poor kid. That woman must be a sack of virulence. Is Diane pushing you aside?"

"No. She has been great and Mom—she has even been talking about our wedding plans! Isn't that something? She was so bent out of shape before that she just froze at the mention of it. This has been cathartic for both her and Randy. I guess it had to be done. Now they don't feel tied to their mother and realize that it isn't them who failed, but her."

"Well Saints in all their Glory!" Mo rejoiced, "It surely has taken the best part of an eon for that to come about! Oh, here is your brother."

"Where's my comic book?" Ian asked as he took the phone.

"I don't have it. You squirreled it away. It serves you right that you forgot where you put it."

"How yah doing?" Ian asked seriously. "We had quite a time keeping Uncle Egan and Carl under control here. And Mom, she was out loading her arsenal! How did such a nice guy grow up in this family of hooligans?"

"You mean me? I was always special."

"No doorknob, I meant me. You get in and out of more messes than Rain! Just wait until you see her Matt? She is so wound up about going to work on Darrell's farm this summer, I can't believe it."

"I'm anxious to see her."

"Yah, she was marching with the color guard last night! And Father Vicaro! You would have thought he was about to lead the Crusades! I guess all these folks don't know what a sap you really are."

Matt got serious, "No, I guess they don't. It is really an awful feeling knowing someone planned to take action to make you dead. It isn't like a war where it isn't personal. I mean you still end up as dead, but she hates me so much she worked out all the details to kill me."

"I've heard other people mention that feeling. When we get shot at in the line of duty it was more like the Army. I have talked to others who were the victims of pre-mediation like this and they all say what you said. You will be able to handle it. You have common sense and remember, you have many folks that do care about you. Oh, by the way, Darrell has only called here a dozen times. If you can, you might want to give him a call."

"I thought about doing that. Tell everyone I love them and I am going to call Jessup. You know, he is a good friend."

"Take care, hey? Do you guys know when you will be able to leave?"

"Not yet. We are supposed to know today. We will call. I hope we can have some time to see everyone there."

The phone rang a couple times before it was answered, "Hello, this is Jessups."

"What were you doing, sleeping" Matt chuckled.

"Matt! How are you man? I was so worried. I mean every one kept me informed, but I was going crazy. You know, it is hard to find a good farm hand!"

"I miss you. I would say I wish you could be here, but it has been a fright. I should get out of the hospital today. I tell you, I didn't take more than a couple bites of that sandwich and I was seeing the hereafter!"

"I never knew you were that allergic to clams!"

"I got sick before and wheezed, but not this bad. The doctor said that was because of two things. One it builds up in your system or something and she had laced my sandwich with four ounces of clam juice!"

"She wasn't messing around, huh?"

"No, she wanted me dead. It would be hard to prove in court, but we know that she did. I can't wait to get home."

"How is Tinker doing?" Darrell asked.

"Diane is doing okay. This seems to have helped both her and Randy put the situation with her Mom in perspective. Bea is in a cast for three months."

"I can't imagine how that must hurt. It makes the hair stand up on the back of my neck to think of getting whacked with a metal bar across your shins! That woman has to be certifiable."

"You wouldn't believe her. I think she could have held her own against Earl Waggoner. Hey, I have to get off the phone. My phone bill will be bigger than my hospital bill. Tell Jeannie I love her and give Joallyn a hug for me. How are things going? Clarence said he is doing a good job with the pets! He had to tell me he earned his other baby goat!"

"Yes, he was so excited. Now he owns Hansel and Gretel. He has taken very good care of your pets and you know how he is, such a worrywart. He calls me a couple times a day to see if they are okay."

"Sounds like our boy. Oh, I hear congratulations are in order! You guys are going to be Clarence's Godparents. That's fantastic."

"Yah. Clarissa picked you and Tink I hear. That must make us related somehow, uh?"

"No, Darrell. I don't think so."

"Yah, I think we are Godparents once-removed."

"If you say so. Bye Darrell."


Randy, Bea and Diane were back to the motel from breakfast before eight o'clock when the detectives called. Arrangements were made to all meet at the hospital about nine-thirty, so they could sign their statements.

At eight-thirty, the kids' attorney called and said he was on his way over to meet with Mrs. Berg. He would stop at the motel on his way, so the kids could sign the document.

Father Sebastian called right after the attorney hung up. "I received a call from Shorepoint this morning. You mom was very distraught when the detectives left and they had to call the attendants. She had a mild relaxer, but she asked that I be called. I was surprised because last night, there was no question in her mind that she wanted nothing to do with me."

"She is pretty good at showing folks the door," Randy said. "Are you going over?"

"Yes, I promised her I would. Last night I think she was denying it to herself, but I wonder if she isn't beginning to see what a huge mess she created. She will need someone there."

"How come don't folks realize how far that can go before they shoot their wad? She has herself in a doozy of a mess this time."

"How are you all doing?"

"Good. On our way over to the hospital soon to see when Matt can leave. Father, I know I was snappy yesterday, but I really do appreciate you taking an interest in our mom."

"No problem, Randy," Father Sebastian said. "That's my job. Talk to you later."

Mr. Bennett knocked on Loretta Berg's door. He wondered about this woman whose children had become his newest clients. A priest answered the door, "Hello, I am Father Sebastian from St. Ignatius."

"I know you. I have grandchildren going to St. Ignatius and they are on the hockey team." the man said as he extended his hand. "I am John Bennett, the attorney retained by Mrs. Berg's children. I came to present and explain some papers to Mrs. Berg."

"Come in. We are expecting you. I'm here to help Mrs. Berg handle some of the things that are going on."

"Good idea." The man came in and extended his hand to the frail woman in the wheelchair. "Hello, Loretta Berg?"

"Yes. I suppose you are here to pile on to all the destruction my offspring are heaping on me! I can't believe what they are doing."

"I imagine you might look at it that way," the man said as he sat at the table. "I have some papers for you to look over."

"I won't sign a damned thing! I want to leave everything the way it is!"

"You can't. Your agreement is not necessary for this to be in effect. It was action taken on their part. They transferred your moneys to Portland Bank and Trust. However, if you don't want their trust officer to handle it, you may appoint your own. Do you have legal representation?"

"No. I don't need anyone."

"You might want to consider getting some. I understand that you could be facing charges through the police department and you will need some then. Also, you will want to have someone look over the papers about the trust money. It may be necessary for you to access some of your funds. It is my understanding that you have to move and coupled with the impending criminal charges, you need assistance."

"I am not moving anywhere! These vultures here just want more money. That's all. They won't make me move."

"I'm sorry, but I have a copy of the letter sent to your son. It was copied to you, so I'm sure you have a copy."

"I throw all that junk away. It is Randy's job to take care of it. I'm his mother and he owes it to me."

"He has released himself from these obligations. Here is the paperwork."

The woman grabbed the papers and began to shuffle through them, becoming more and more agitated. "This is ridiculous! They can't do this! Why do they want a restraining order? I don't live anywhere near them! They are being overly-dramatic."

Father Sebastian motioned to the papers, "May I?"

"Knock yourself out." Then she scowled at Bennett, "You did your deed, now get lost."

"I need to have you sign that you received and understood these papers," Bennett said calmly. "I think it would be wise for you to get an attorney."

"You can be my attorney!"

"No, I cannot. I represent your children. However, I can give you the phone numbers of two legal firms in town. I would suggest one of them. They handle civil and criminal law. I think you should talk to them and do it soon."

Father Sebastian nodded, "Mrs. Berg, he is right."

"Can't Randy come and find me one? Why can't the kids find me a place to stay and an attorney? Why not?" she began to cry.

"Do you understand, Ma'am?" Bennett repeated, "They want no further contact with you."

"How long? They'll get over it. I know they will."

"It sounded rather permanent to me," Bennett repeated. "I'm glad you have Father Sebastian here. Could you please sign this receipt for me and I will be on my way?"

"Give me the damned thing. I will sign it and when you give it to them, tell those poor excuses for humanity that I want nothing to do with them! So there! I have always hated them both. I'm sorry I brought them into this world," she snarled.

"I wish you the best and I will give the names of those law firms to Father Sebastian. Please reconsider."

"Get lost."

Bennett stood up and gathered his papers. He shook Father Sebastian's hand and said, "Please try to talk her into calling someone."

There was a knock at the door and they all jumped. Father Sebastian opened the door to find two uniformed police standing there. Bennett looked at Mrs. Berg, "You need to make that call now."

She stared at the uniforms without any reaction. Bennett nodded at the officers and then told Father, "If she won't call, you should."

The doctor came in to see Matt and gave him the good news, "Everything is looking good. Here are some prescriptions you should fill right away. We are still waiting for a few blood tests and if they are okay, the nurse will let you know and you can leave."

"Thank you."

"You are welcome, Matt. Good luck and I hope you can find some time to relax on your vacation."

"Have a great Easter."

Randy, Bea and Diane came into the room. "What did he say?"

"I just have to wait for the results of a couple tests and I can go. What have you been doing?"

While Randy was explaining their morning, Mr. Bennett came in. He gave them the copies of the work he had taken to their mom. Then he explained how it went. "It looks like the police are taking her in for questioning. Two uniformed policemen were there as I left."

Diane turned pale and sat down. Bea took Randy's hand and asked, "Is Loretta doing okay?"

"She is very belligerent. I think it is beginning to sink in. Father Sebastian was there with her."

"That's good," Bea said.

"Well, if you need to contact me, you can call my service. We are having family at our place over Easter, so I will be around. I certainly want to talk to you before you leave town. Oh, I gave Father Sebastian the numbers of a couple law firms she should contact. She is going to need someone to help her through the maze of decisions she needs to make."

"Thank you so much," Randy said. "I appreciate how fast you got everything done of us."

"Yes, thank you," Diane said.

As he was heading out the door, the two Detectives came in. "Am I being tailed?" Bennett chuckled. "Two cops just came in as I was leaving the last place I was at!"

Eastman winked, "We are on to you, Bennett."

"Good bye all," Bennett said as he left. "Have a nice Easter."

"I thought you were at Shorepoint. Bennett said the police were knocking on Mom's door. I figured it was you." Randy said.

"No, we sent two uniforms out to bring her in for questioning. We came here to get you to sign your statements. Read them over carefully and if there are any changes, tell us right away. Then we can get back to the station," Eastman explained.

Lauer explained further, "We went over everything with the assistant DA. They aren't too eager to take the case although they think that she is guilty as sin. The DA is running for re-election and this wouldn't look good in the newspaper. However, they agree that she should be brought in and questioned. If we can get her to admit to more than she has so far, we can charge her."

"Did she admit to something?" Diane asked.

"She admits she ran into Bea, but maintains it was an accident. She slipped and named clam juice as the poison on the sandwich, but she didn't admit she did it. That is what we would like. Short of that, we might not go anywhere with it, but we aren't letting her know that. Without an admission she attempted to murder Mr. Harrington, the most she would likely get is probation of some kind."

"She was right," Bea exclaimed. "She said she could get away with it."

"Now don't worry dear, we will try to get her to spill the beans. When she gets angry, she says things that are of no help to her," Lauer said. "I just hope we have time before she gets a lawyer."

"I think she is getting one."

"Figured as much, but we will talk to her first, if we can," Eastman smiled at Matt. "Looks like you are checking out soon, huh?"

Matt answered, "Just waiting for some lab work. Here are papers."

Everyone handed their signed statements back to the detectives. Lauer smiled, "Well, we are off. We will call either here or the motel when we find out? Okay? I'm sure you are anxious to know what is going on."

"We are," Randy said. "I guess those lab tests won't be done for another hour and a half, so call us here before then. Thanks."

# 15

The police had their hands full getting Mrs. Berg to the patrol car. It was similar to trying to put a cat in a running shower! It took the police officers, two Shorepoint attendants, Dr. Werner and Father Sebastian to get her into the backseat.

As the car drove off, Dr. Werner looked at Father Sebastian, "That was a first! I sure hope it will be the last."

"Anyone who thinks she is weak should have seen her a bit ago. I don't think that I could fight off that many. Well, I suppose I should call an attorney for her and then go down to the police station."

Werner nodded, "Yes, and she had a mild tranquilizer a short time ago. When it wears off, they will need all the help they can get!"

They both stood watching the taillights disappear around the corner, before they went inside. Finally Werner asked, "Do you think that she in any way thinks she is responsible for any of this?"

"I doubt she cares." Sebastian shook his head, "Do you think she can handle it emotionally or physically?"'

"Depends. She won't need another tranquilizer for a couple more hours. Then I can't predict if she will flip out."

"How much more can she flip?" the priest asked.

"I have no idea. You can make your call from my office."

Father Sebastian was finally able to reach one of the law firms. It took some explaining, but he did get someone from Branson, Branson and Fitz to say they would send someone down to the station. He asked that the priest would meet him there.

"I imagine I should go down there now. Mr. Fitz will meet me there in about half an hour."

When Detective Lauer and Detective Eastman arrived at the station, Mrs. Berg was sitting in an interrogation room. The policeman who was sitting outside of the door looked at them and grimaced, "Better make sure your rabies shots are up to date! She wasn't even arrested, only brought in for questioning. What a viper!"

"Yes, we have seen it. Did she throw herself out of the wheelchair and on to the floor?"

"No. They were looking for tarp straps to keep her in it. Poor O'Donnell picked her out of the chair to set her into the patrol car! He is wondering if he will be able to have children now! You should charge her with assaulting a police officer, but none of us want her around."

"I know," Eastman said. "One of the things were are asking her about is driving into her daughter-in-law to be with that wheelchair. The girl is a ballerina and she cracked the bone in her shin!"

The officer shook his head, "I'm gonna go home and kiss my mom."

Lauer chuckled, "You should have been doing that anyway."

"I know, but this woman shows how bad life could be!"

The two detectives walked into the gray room each carrying their coffee mugs. Mrs. Berg was sitting in her wheelchair. It was secured to the table with handcuffs on each table leg. It would be impossible for her to move the chair or throw herself out of it. The tiny woman was disheveled and hateful. One could almost see the fumes rising from her small frame. When the detectives sat down, Lauer turned on the tape recorder and stated the date and who was present.

"This place is filthy! Which derelicts do you hire to clean around here? A person could get sick just being here!" Mrs. Berg snarled. "This place should be condemned."

"Talk to your city commission," Eastman smiled. "We kinda like it. Trust me, it grows on you."

"What the hell do you think you are doing? Dragging me in here like a common criminal?" Mrs. Berg demanded, her nostrils flaring.

"Assault and murder are crimes," Lauer stated flatly. "You better get this through your head, sweetheart. People in wheelchairs, walkers and crutches do go to prison. Convicts in wheelchairs either manually operate them themselves or are pushed around by other prisoners. If you talk to them like you talk to the attendants at Shorepoint, you'd be in a world of uglies real quick. They won't tolerate that."

Loretta glared at her and tried to conceal her surprise. She hadn't known that. She had never imagined that there were invalids in prison. Well, it didn't matter, because she would never have to go there. She knew how to worm out of this mess.

"You won't ever be able to send me to prison, you obese cow! It was an accident that I ran into Bea and you can never prove differently," Loretta stated smugly.

"Do you want an attorney present?" Mike Eastman asked.

"Hell no, those bottom feeders are about as dumb as you are. I can handle this myself."

"Now," Eastman began, "We were speaking about Mr. Harrington's sandwich. We have signed statements that you ordered and received a bottle of clam juice that morning. It was with the groceries."

"It is not a crime to order clam juice."

"Why did you order it?"

"I like it."

"Cute, what did you want to use it for?" Lauer asked.

"For Bloody Marys. You can put some in the drink for flavor," Loretta responded calmly. "Lots of people do it."

"We found the empty bottle of clam juice in your trash. You used it all?"

"How did you get my trash?"

"From maintenance. You drank an entire four ounce bottle of clam juice before eleven AM?"

"So, what's it too you?"

"You better tell us because it doesn't matter to either of us if you bathed in it. You are the one who needs the plausible explanation," Eastman said with authority.

She glared at him and decided that she was beginning to intensely dislike him. "I forgot. A friend borrowed it."

Lauer smiled, "Okay. We need your friend's name."

"I can't remember it."

"You better remember, because the only fingerprints on the bottle were yours and those of the delivery boy. His got there when you asked him to open the bottle for you."

Loretta had never considered they would do fingerprinting! They must have questioned everyone. That wasn't good. She felt the tension build in her spine, but knew she had to keep calm to control this conversation. She took a deep breath.

"I guess that was another time. I made myself a big drink after that fiasco at the meeting. I had a Bloody Mary with clam juice."

"There was only about a shot out of the vodka bottle and no tomato juice. That must have been some Bloody Mary."

Even though she could feel her chest tighten, she didn't want to let them see her weakness. Her look riveted the young man, "You should try it sometime."

Lauer cleared her throat, "We established earlier than you knew which sandwich was for Harrington, and you even checked to make certain the sandwiches would be labeled. You were alone in the consulting room with the sandwiches for at least ten minutes. You had more than enough time to lace Harrington's sandwich with the juice. No one else had the opportunity."

"What about the delivery guy? He was alone with the sandwiches," Loretta pointed out. "He might have done it."

"Why? He didn't even know Harrington."

"Did you ask him? How do you know?"

"We did and he'd never met him." Eastman moved his papers, "Look, you have motive, opportunity and we know you planned it. We know you broke Bea Fedder's leg and tried to murder Matthew Harrington."

"Tried?" The skinny woman's eyes flew open and she screeched, "You mean the bastard isn't dead? I have gone through all this and he's still alive! How in the hell did that happen? I put enough juice on that sandwich to choke an elephant! And he isn't even dead! Is there no God?"

The detectives looked at the hysterical woman. She began to hyperventilate and grabbed at her own throat. They went to the phone to call for medical assistance. A team came running in as the detectives had removed the handcuffs from the chair.

Once the wheelchair was moved away from the table, Loretta threw herself onto the concrete floor. She only screamed one profanity before she went quiet. They were giving the woman oxygen as her attorney Mr. Fitz and Father Sebastian entered the station.

The medics put her on a gurney to take her to the hospital. "She needs to be evaluated. Her blood pressure was sky high. She may have had a massive stroke, or received a cerebral event when she crashed onto the floor, or both! Who should we notify?"

"I will send Officer Pelton to go with her now, and we'll join you as soon as possible. We need to bring her attorney and priest up to speed," Detective Lauer said.

After she was taken to the ambulance, Eastman asked Father Sebastian and Mr. Fitz to come into their office. "What happened?"

Lauer brought the tape recorder and played it for them. The two men were shocked at her behavior. There was silence for a bit before Fitz said, "Remind me to thank Bennett for giving her my card. This is a doozey. She handed it to you, didn't she? She was Mirandized?"

"Yes, by the book."

"What are your plans now?" Fitz asked.

Eastman shrugged, "I guess we have to see what the doctor's say before we proceed. Well, I guess Father Sebastian and I will head down to the hospital. Will you ride with me and fill me in on the way?"

"Certainly. I think I should call her family."

"We will. They are still at the hospital. Then we will meet you there," Lauer said.

The phone rang in Matt's room and he answered, "Yes they are here. Let me hand the phone to Randy."

Detective Lauer told Randy what happened and that their mother was on her way to the hospital. Randy didn't know what to do. He went pale and he mumbled, "We can meet you at emergency."

When he hung up, he explained to the rest what had happened. He looked to Matt, "What should we do?"

"You know what you need to do. Follow your heart, Randy. Go to emergency. This is no time to stand on principle. Diane, you go with. I will meet you there as soon as I get out of here," Matt said in a no non-sense manner.

Bea went with them to the emergency room and Matt sat on his bed and said a prayer.

Matt called Randy and Diane's attorney, who said he would meet them at the hospital. Then he asked the nurse if he could go down to the emergency room. She said she would call his doctor and let him know.

A few minutes later, she popped in, "The doctor said okay, but get dressed in your street clothes first and don't leave the grounds until we get the blood reports back. Oh, and keep on the high class bracelet we gave you, so we know you are ours!"

Matt grinned and got out of bed. He gathered his clothing and took a shower. It felt good to be in street clothes again. He went down the hall to the emergency room.

He found a group he recognized in the waiting room. He went over to Diane and took her hand. She turned and gave him a hug, "Did you get released?"

"Not yet. But they said I could come down here as long as they know where I am. Have you heard anything?"

"No. The doctors are with her," Bea said. "Do you think we should call Mr. Bennett?"

"I already did. He will be here in a bit."

Matt noticed Randy sitting alone staring at the floor. He whispered to Bea, "Is he okay?"

"No. He is blaming himself now. He thinks he might have killed her."

Matt nodded and moved over to sit beside him, "Hi."

Randy looked up, "I should have left it alone. But no, I had to go off like a tyrant and make a big deal about it. Now look."

Matt put his hand on his friend's shoulder, "Hey, I can go out on the patio. Want to come out with me and you can have a cigarette? The girls can call us."

Randy nodded and Matt told the girls. Bea nodded and said softly, "Thanks."

The two men sat at a picnic table in view of the waiting room and Randy lit his cigarette. "What a hell of a week."

"Hey, this is not your fault. You weren't trying to be cruel, you were protecting yourself and your loved ones. That is not wrong. I'm sorry that this happened to her, but the choice was hers. All along. If she had chosen to be even a bit nice, we'd have taken her to North Dakota and made her part of our lives. She didn't want that. She wanted to be the only queen in the palace. Sadly, that never works very well."

"I know, I know, Matt. I also know that if she had a chance, she would do it all over again. Eastman said that she admitted she intended to kill you. You know why she stroked out or whatever?"

"No."

"When she found out that you were still alive! She was so upset that you weren't dead that she had a convulsion! I can't believe it." Then he started to cry.

Matt held his friend who had only tried to do the best for everyone, while he cried as if his heart was broken. Matt rubbed his back and let him sob. After a couple minutes, Randy pulled himself together. He leaned back, wiped his face and took a draw off his cigarette. "I wish Elton was here."

"Yah," Matt agreed. "He is good at this kind of stuff."

The two sat for a minute and then Randy asked, "How does one ever get good at this?"

Matt shrugged, "I guess you face enough stuff, you can get good at anything. Randy, it will be okay. None of this is your fault. There is no way you could let Bea be hurt."

"Or you killed? Do you realize my own mother tried to murder my best friend? What the hell does that make me?"

"It makes you a fine person with a big mess. Dr. Werner, the detectives, the whole bunch find her impossible to deal with. None of us think that you or Diane haven't done as good as job as humanly possible. Now, have you got that?"

"Yah, I got that." Randy put out his cigarette, "I suppose we should get in there. Diane needs you and Bea should have her leg up and rest. Matt, I don't know how much more of this I can take."

"We can do it, together," Matt stated. "I know we can."

As they came back into the waiting room, Dr. Werner came over to them. "I just heard. What did the doctors say?"

"Haven't heard yet," Randy answered.

"I will go see what I can find out."

As Werner left, Mr. Bennett came through the door. "What's been going on?"

They explained what they knew and then Mr. Fitz came over and shook Bennett's hand. "I really want to thank you for this."

"Any time, Fitzie! It is payback for the Norton case."

"Yes, that was a nice one. Could we find a corner and you could fill me in?" Mrs. Berg's attorney asked.

"Sure, there is a spot over there."

Father Sebastian came over, "Nice to see you looking better, Matt. When did they release you?"

"They haven't yet, but said I could get dressed and come down here. They are waiting for a few test results before I get my official walking papers."

"I'm sorry things degenerated so fast, but I'm not surprised. She is certainly a feisty one," the priest said as he moved his sleeve up and showed them the scratches on his wrist. Then he chuckled, "Please don't mention it to the staff at St. Ignatius. I don't want them to know I succumbed in seconds to that little thing. They wouldn't appreciate what it was like."

"I know. She wiped out Bea and me in a heartbeat." Matt agreed.

Diane started to cry softly, "I know, for years no one believed Randy and me. They always acted like we were nutty or something."

"I know Diane, and I was as guilty as the next. Would you accept my sincerest apologies?" Matt put his arm around her. "I simply didn't understand that she backed up her vitriol with cruelty. Was she abusive to you when you were kids?"

"Matt, I don't want to talk about this now. Please."

"You're right. I'm sorry. I should've been more respectful."

Diane kissed his cheek, "Thanks, I love you."

After an hour of milling around and making small talk, a doctor appeared. While he spoke to Randy in particular, everyone else gathered around to hear about Mrs. Berg's condition.

"Mrs. Berg is in stable condition now. She suffered a massive stroke and a concussion when she fell on a concrete floor. That may have actually saved her life because it allowed the blood pressure to be relieved when she bled from her external injury. Right now, she is unable to move or speak. We know she is awake and likely aware of her surroundings. Her eyes can follow movement so we are rather certain she has some visual abilities. Her blood pressure is now stabilized. She won't be able to see any guests right now, but she can see family for a minute or her clergy."

"This is Detective Lauer. Do you know what her prognosis is or when you will know?"

"We won't know for certain for at least twenty-hour hours. A full recovery is unlikely, but the degree of recovery will simply take time to determine. She is relatively young, but has not been active for years. We understand that she suffered some brain damage about fifteen years ago with the meningitis, so she did not start out with a healthy brain."

"Is she able to eat or swallow?" Dr. Werner asked.

"Not at this time. She will have a gastric feeding tube until she regains that ability."

"Would that be in the near future?" Mr. Fitz asked. "I am her attorney."

"We don't know, but not within a month or so," the doctor explained. "She will remain in the hospital for some time, but it would be a considerable time before she might be able to return to Shorepoint. She will need constant care."

Diane sat down and put her head in her hands. Matt sat next to her and put her arms around her while they listened.

"There were some pending criminal charges against her," Fitz explained. "Will it be feasible for her to take any part in any of her defense or make decisions for her own care?"

"Not for some time, if ever. I'm sorry to be vague, but a lot will depend on the next day or so. She may not improve at all."

"Thank you, Doctor," Randy said.

"Any other questions, please feel free to contact me. If you want to come see her, let the nurse know. Only stay a minute," the doctor said as he shook his hand.

The detectives came over and told the kids they would be meeting with the DA and both attorneys to work out some sort of agreement. Then Dr. Werner offered to check into facilities that could take over her care. I will call you, Mr. Fitz or Father Sebastian with the information this afternoon. I'm so sorry at these turn of events."

After everyone else scattered, Father Sebastian came over. "I think I will go see her now. Do you want to?"

They all shrugged, but it was Diane who answered, "She probably hates us even worse now. I doubt she would want to see us."

"I suggest that I go see her and then I'll come talk to you, in Matt's room?"

"Yes, we will go back there now. Let us know."

The four walked down the hall. In the room, Bea sat down and put her leg up in the recliner. Matt sat on his bed and Diane sat on the chair. Randy paced the floor in circles.

"Randy, take a deep breath. You need to calm down." Matt said, "You do what you feel is right. Don't worry about what anyone else thinks. You too, Diane. It is your mother. You have every right to see her or not, as you feel."

"I think I want to talk to that doctor," Randy said, "Coming with, Sis?"

"Yes. I have a few more things I'd like to find out. Okay Matt?"

He kissed his fiancée and said, "It is fine. Bea and I will be here."

Bea leaned back in the recliner and said, "I don't know what I'd do. I wish I could help Randy more. He is so tortured about this. He feels guilty for everything."

"I know he does. He hasn't yet realized that this is his mother's legacy to him. She planted the guilt years ago. I hope he can shake it. I watched Diane vacillate repeatedly with her guilt. She finds it much easier to attack anyone other than her mother. It is amazing."

"I know about some of it. Randy said you've been through the mill. May I ask you something that is quite impertinent?"

Matt smiled, "Of course. What is it?"

"Have you ever wondered if you are making a mistake marrying Diane, because of all this baloney?"

Matt took her hand, "Honestly, I have. I still do. I know that I love her and she loves me and I really hate to blame her for what her mother did. That would be the ultimate victory for her mom. Sometimes I think I am out of my mind to even consider it. How about you?'

"Yes, I have. Like you said, Randy and I love each other. When something about this comes up, he simply withdraws. He is aware that he does and always apologizes, but sometimes I feel very alone. I don't understand how to help him or what to do."

Matt hugged her, "I know. I have been there myself more often than I care to admit. But when she and I are apart, I can hardly stand it. I have an idea. When you can't take it anymore, call me. We can commiserate."

Bea hugged him back, "I will if you do. You would likely never call me. You have it so together."

Matt laughed, "Not really! I promise; I will call. Please know too, Bea that if you can't handle it, I would understand. It wasn't even a week ago I was ready to break up with Diane again!"

Bea just broke out in gales of laughter! "Me, too! Now look! We came that close to avoiding being maimed! Life is funny, if you think about it."

"That's what I love about you! You have the best attitude. I get all morose and melancholy. We'll do okay, my friend. We will do just all right!"

"I think we will. Maybe I should write my memoirs while I am waiting for my shin to heal!"

"Don't you have to be older, to write your memoirs?"

"Maybe so, huh? Well, we'd better rest. I have a feeling we are going to be needed before this day is done."

"You need your pain pill?"

"Not 'til noon."

Randy and Diane were able to talk to Dr. Levinson alone. He had a smattering of Loretta's recent history and welcomed the new information. "With all that going on, I would have high blood pressure, too. She certainly has herself in a dreadful jam, doesn't she?"

"Yes, she does. We don't wish her ill, I hope you understand that. We just couldn't be around her anymore," Diane said. "I don't know if she would want to see us."

"Your reaction seems very sensible to me. I have no idea how she would feel about seeing you; since she has sent very conflicting signals. The priest is with her now, and maybe you would like to talk to him. She is pretty doped up now, and I really don't want to throw a monkey wrench in the works, so I would suggest that you put off seeing her at least until tonight. Can you do that?"

"Yes. We need to find her a place to live also."

"There isn't a rush about that on our end, but since you are leaving, it will be. I want you to be aware that she may never make it out of here. However, she is a determined fighter and that will serve her well. She may surprise us all. Call me before you go see her, okay?"

The nurse came in and told Matt he was cleared to leave. He went down to sign the insurance papers while Bea gathered their things. The phone rang and it was Dr. Werner, "If you can stop by, I have a list of facilities you might want to check out."

"I will tell them," Bea said.

She hung up and sighed. She jumped when she felt arms around her. Then Matt said in her ear, "It will be okay, Bea. I just know it."

She turned around and gave him a kiss on the cheek. "I know it, too. Nobody promised a rose garden!"

"Hey, did I ever tell you about my begonia?"

"You didn't, but I've heard about it. Most people think it has been dead for two years. Do you honestly think it will bloom?" Bea giggled.

"Yes, I do. I know it will. It is just really dormant," Matt replied seriously.

Bea looked at him and winked, "Okay then. I'm looking forward to seeing it!"

# 16

The four walked down to find Father Sebastian who was coming their way. He smiled, "I guess they sprung you, huh Matthew?"

"Yes, just minutes ago. We thought we would go get some lunch and then head over to Shorepoint. Want to join us? I'm buying!" Matt offered.

"My favorite words, if everyone doesn't just want to be away from me for a bit."

"No, please. Join us. We are tired of us anyway, and would relish someone new to harass," Bea giggled.

"I can't pass that up. Where too?"

"You live here, you name a place. A cheap place," Matt grinned.

"There is a nice family restaurant on the way to Shorepoint. It is called Bussells. Funny name, but good food. It is just down on Forest Avenue."

"Meet you there," Randy said. "I'd offer you a ride, but you'd have to ride on the hood."

"Haven't done that since I was a teenager," Sebastian grinned.

Inside the restaurant, they sat in a large, overstuffed vinyl corner booth. They took the menus from behind the shiny napkin dispenser and passed them around. The waitress in the freshly pressed uniform and apron came over with iced water. She said she'd would be back to take their order.

Randy looked around, "This is a really nice place. I like it."

"It is my favorite," Father Sebastian said. "The food is very good and not expensive."

"I noticed," Matt chuckled. "I am so hungry. However, I have to admit I am a little nervous about eating anything."

After their food came and Matt said grace, they began to eat. Bea was the first to bring up the subject, "Dr. Werner said he had a few places that could care for Loretta. He was going to talk to Mr. Fitz about it, too. He would be the one to make the decision and let the trust officer know."

"I wonder what they are going to do with all that. I should have just kept my mouth shut for a while. We could take care of things," Randy mumbled to himself.

Father Sebastian nodded seriously, "No, I think you did the only thing you could do. She admitted that she intended to kill Matt and I'm certain she broke Bea's leg on purpose. She was disappointed that she only broke one leg. It is one thing to forgive that sort of behavior and quite another to allow it to continue. You had no choice. Shorepoint had no choice, either. They couldn't let one of the patients get away with that. It is too bad and she is in a horrible situation, but she worked hard to get there. She didn't do it overnight, either. She earned it over time."

"Could you communicate with her?"

"She was drowsy, but she did manage to give me a dirty look. I prayed for her. She glared at me. Then I told her that you were there and wished her the best. I believe she had a tear, but I wasn't certain. I talked for a while and she seemed expressionless until I said I had to leave. She looked at me with a bit of fear. When I told her I would be back, the look went away. I think she is terrified to be alone. Now she is with herself. That is a creation of her own making that wouldn't be fun to be around." The priest finished buttering his roll and noticed they were all staring at him. "What did I say?"

"Thank you so much for that. You have no idea how much better that makes me feel. I was beating myself up about all this," Randy said.

"I deserve no credit. It simply is the situation. I guess that is one of the reasons we should try to live a good life. So, if we are ever trapped in our own bodies, we can tolerate ourselves."

"Good point," Matt said. "I imagine it gives a person a lot of time to think things over and rethink them; with little chance of changing anything."

"It may take her awhile, but I hope that she can begin to understand the effect of her actions. I won't give up on her. I promised her I'll come and visit her. She needs that now; even though she hates it. I could just about imagine what was going through her head while I was talking to her. I knew she was thinking of a hundred foul names to call me!"

"Doesn't that bother you?" Diane asked.

"Not at all. I wish she wouldn't be like that, but that is the spirit that will keep her fighting. Now if we can get her to use it to join the world instead of attack it, we will be on a good track."

On the way to Shorepoint, the folks in the Toyota decided that Loretta had a good ally in Father Sebastian. They also decided they would attend Good Friday services at St. Ignatius the next day.

"Can I take a bit of down time this afternoon?" Bea asked. "I really need a nap and I know Diane needs to go shopping for a dress for that little girl. Randy should go blow off some steam."

"Okay, let's plan on it. I saw a place on the Back Bay where we could rent a motor boat by the hour? Could I convince someone to go out with me for an hour?" Randy asked.

"I will," Matt said. "I could use some fresh air."

"Me, too," Diane said. "If I don't get Clarissa's dress today, I can later."

"I will too, if you let me take a nap first," Bea smiled. "Like half an hour."

"Seriously, I think we could all use a good rest."

At Shorepoint, Fitz and Werner were going over the brochures for convalescent care homes in Portland when they arrived. Dr. Werner had them all sit down, "Glad you got here. We wondered if maybe you would prefer to move her to the Dakotas?"

"No," Diane answered immediately. "We live over an hour from Bismarck and Merton has a retirement home, but you have to be rather fit to live there. That would be silly to move her there."

"Besides, I'm not so certain her health would permit a major move like that for some time," Randy stated. "It is best to keep her here. If things change down the road, we can change things. I am stationed in Dover, Delaware until October. So I will be close by if something happens."

"That is about what we thought. Well, there is Portland Convalescent Care or St. Jude's Convalescent Home. Those are the only two that take patients in your Mom's condition."

"What are they like?" Diane asked.

Mr. Fitz answered, "Neither are as nice as Shorepoint. Of course, if you can't get out of bed, having a view isn't as necessary. PCC is adequate and if she survives more than a few years, the county will maintain her with her Medicare and Social Security. It is grim, but safe and clean. St. Jude's is more expensive and a bit nicer. However, once her funds run out, she will have to be transferred to PCC."

"How long can she afford St. Jude's Home?" Matt asked.

"About two years," Fitz determined. "Of course, I have to talk to the trust officer, but that is about it. Some of it depends on if either of you plan on suing Mrs. Berg in a civil case. You would both have a good case. Then the money could be drawn out to pay the claim and she would go on aid right away."

"I have no intention of suing her," Matt said right away.

"Me, either," Bea said. "I see no reason why she shouldn't just pay to take care of herself as long as she can."

"Good." Fitz nodded, "My suggestion would be to put her in St. Jude's. We have no idea how long she will survive."

Dr. Werner put in, "St. Jude's has a great physical therapy department. That would be my choice. If she makes it as long as two years, it will mean she has worked on her rehab. Then she could live a long time."

"Do you think she will?"

"I haven't been right once when it came to her," Dr. Werner shrugged. "But I know she really let her body waste away for a long time. She would have a mighty climb to get back to getting around on her own. I would say it would be unlikely she will ever."

"Well, Sis? Does that sound reasonable to you?"

"Yes, she will have it as good as she can as long as she can afford it. When that is over, it is over. She could have been out in the world like everyone else all these years. She chose to be waited on and she was. You know, she always wanted every little thing done for her. Now she will have that. I guess you should be careful what you wish for."

At the motel, Bea crashed on the bed in the girl's room. Her pain pill was late, so she was hurting by the time she took it. Randy lay down beside her and while they were talking, they both fell asleep.

Diane and Matt took the car and went down to the shops in Portland. They were fortunate that so many places had their Easter dresses on display. In one window was a mother-daughter set that had an old-fashioned dress with three quarter sleeves with lace on the bottom. The bodice had a long four-inch lace gathered across the top and the same lace was tiered in three sections in the skirt. The dresses were cream colored, but there were tiny pink roses scattered on the lace.

Diane had the happiest smile Matt had seen in some time when she saw it. "I think this is it! Do you think she will be very upset that it isn't all pink?"

Matt grinned, "If it is soft, you might get away with it. Let's go look."

They went inside and asked to see the dresses. They were a very soft acrylic and even the lace was soft. Matt suggested that they could get Clarissa some pink ribbons for her hair and the clerk overheard him. "Is this for Easter?"

"No, she is getting baptized the week after. It is her christening dress."

"I have a darling little hat that would match it. The hat is white but has a pink ribbon and one side has several of those same pink flowers on the brim. Would you like to see it?"

"We would."

They looked at it and other than the fact that she would have to take it off during the actual baptism; they decided it would be perfect. The couple bought it and left the store. On their way back to the car, they bought souvenirs. Diane took great glee in buying Elton a tee shirt with a humungous lobster on it.

Matt shook his head, "Diane, he wanted at real lobster."

Diane giggled, "I know. He'll get over it. This it much more meaningful!"

"You can do that, but I value my life. I want to stop when we come back from our boat trip. I saw a place that ships lobsters all over the country."

"Brown-noser!" Diane giggled.

Matt stopped walking and took her hand, "I love you."

Diane kissed his cheek, "Let's get back to the motel. I don't think we need to get arrested for indecent exposure!"

"Why would that happen?" Matt flashed a sly grin.

"We might want to take a nap." She giggled, "Do you remember when you asked me to make out with you in the hospital in front of a room full of people?"

Matt stepped back, "I didn't. Did I?"

"You were real dopey and they just brought you back to your room. Actually, I guess it was only Randy and Bea there."

"Bit of difference from what you first said."

"I know," Diane giggled as she got in the car. "Let's go home."

There was no nap. When they arrived back at the room, Randy was on the phone. It was soon apparent he was speaking with the detectives. After several minutes, he hung up.

"What was that about?" Diane asked.

"Can we go outside? I would like Bea to be able to sleep and I want a cigarette."

They walked over to the bench that overlooked a flower garden and sat down. Randy of course, paced while he lit his cigarette. "That was Lauer. I guess they had a big pow-wow with the DA, Fitz and Bennett. Fitz, acting on Mom's behalf, will accept a no contest plea for malicious mischief. She will be on probation for twelve months. Even she should be able to handle that considering she is incapacitated."

"I would think so," Matt agreed.

"I feel bad that she basically got away with it. You guys suffered at her hand and she can skate," Randy grumbled.

"Not really Randy. She is in her own jail now. One that she built herself and the worst part is that she knows it! She didn't skate at all."

"No, I guess not. Do you think we should go see her?"

"Depending on what the doctor and Father Sebastian say, yes I do. You may never get another chance to speak to her. I think that you both really need to do that. Think over what you want to say, because it may be your last chance," Matt said thoughtfully.

"You really think so?"

"Yes," Matt said.

Diane started twisting a tissue in her hand, "I might want to call Samuels first."

"Good idea." Matt said, as he took the shredded tissue from her hand. Then he looked at her quizzically, "May I ask, where do you get these? Do you always have a shredded tissue handy?"

Diane giggled, "I stuff my bra with them every morning!"

Randy shook his head, "You guys are wacky."

After Bea woke from her nap, they went boating for an hour. Then they bought lobster for Elton and Matt rented a car to drive to Boston. They hoped to leave either the next day or Saturday. Bea and Randy would go home and Matt and Diane would have Easter Sunday in Boston and then fly out early the next day.

"Your vacation really got messed up," Randy started. "I'm so-"

Matt pointed at him and exclaimed, "Finish that sentence at your peril! You don't apologize for family business. Stop it!"

Randy raised his eyebrows and steeped back, "Boy, are you cranky!"

"I forgot to tell you, Matt gets a little funny about apologies. He has a limit on them."

"Yah," Matt grinned, "Fifteen times is about all I want to hear of it."

"You keep track?"

"I sure do!" he laughed. "Okay, are you going to see your Mom tonight?"

"No. I need to get away from it a bit. Tomorrow I will. Oh, I better call Samuels," Diane said.

That evening, the two couples went out for a nice quiet dinner and didn't mention the current mess one time.

"Have you set your wedding date yet?" Diane asked.

"Not yet. We want you guys to be in our wedding and Bart to marry us. I don't want to have a cast. So, I guess it will be at least three months. Randy will be out of the Air Force in October. By then we will know if he got the job at the Bismarck Airport."

"Really? How cool." Diane said.

"If not there, I have an application in Minot, too."

"That would be great."

Bea started to say something, and then stopped. Then she said, "Oh what the heck? When are you guys tying the knot?"

"I think June. What about you Matt?" Diane took his hand.

"Sounds good to me."

"We have to get married before Elton and Nora go on their trip to the Grand Caymans. How soon can you come out?"

"We can't likely before we move there. I have used up so much time with this and Bea's schedule is all messed up. You guys listen though, I want you to get married when it is convenient for you. Don't worry about me," Randy said.

"What about me? Maybe I want to be in it? You big dumbbell!" Bea whacked him, "No really, Randy is right. You do it whenever you can."

"We would like you to be in our wedding party," Matt said.

"If you want to wait until I get my cast off, it will be at least three months! No, you guys stand up for us. That will be just fine. Okay?"

"How about if it looks like you can make it, you can be in the party and if not, we will get married anyway?" Matt suggested.

"That works."

The next morning, they got ready and went to early Mass. They spoke with Father Sebastian after the service. "I saw her last night, but she will still very dopey. I plan to see her after the last Mass today. I will scope it out if she wants to see you. You know, I think you should whether she likes it or not. It could be the last time."

"That's what Matt said," Randy said. "We are holding up the line, but call us if you get the time. We plan on leaving town tomorrow."

"I will do that. Have a good day."

Everything was very quiet the rest of the morning. The group went to visit their father's grave where his children placed flowers. They had never been there and, though it was very emotional, they were glad to be able to finally tell him goodbye.

After lunch, they returned to the motel and called Loretta's doctor. They had a message from Dr. Werner and went to see him.

"Mr. Fitz and I got things lined up with St. Jude's. I thought maybe you'd like to decide what to do with her things. Then we can close out her room, transfer her things to St. Jude's and she will get some money back from here. She will need it."

The young people went into her room with Dr. Werner. They all looked around. It was amazing that the woman had not one photo or trinket; nothing that made her an individual. Her clothes and toiletries were packed and sent to St. Jude's. The kids decided to dispose of any foodstuffs and that was all that was there.

At one point, Diane stood looking over the room. It was a beautiful room. The walls were a soft mauve with a darker mauve carpet and drapes. A white sheer covered the sliding glass door to her own patio and the small window above her 'kitchen' sink. She had a small counter for groceries, snack and plates. Under the counter was a small refrigerator. There was a wall that separated the kitchenette from the sleeping area. There she had a large hospital bed complete with a gorgeous bedspread and a full bathroom off to the side. The bed overlooked the living area, which had a table in front of the window, a television and settee with two matching rockers.

"What is it, Honey?" Matt asked.

"Why couldn't she be happy here? This is a beautiful place. Look what she has done."

"I don't know," he said. "I doubt that she knows."

Before they went to dinner, they went over to St. Jude's. They went on a tour and it seemed well-operated. It was an older building and each room only had one small window. It was clean, but much more like a hospital than a home.

"Mom would have a fit if she was in better condition," Diane pointed out.

"Maybe so, but this place is not built for living in. It is more a nursing home."

"I know. Don't know why they can't use a color other an institutional green."

Randy poked Matt and they had a good chuckle about a previous discussion on institutional green. Bea shook her head, "You guys are weird. Come on Diane, let's get away from them."

For dinner, they returned to Bussell's, and had a wonderful meal. Bea said quietly, "You know, I hope I learned something from this."

"What would that be?" Matt asked.

"To appreciate what I have and to try to build memories I can live with."

"Good thought."

"Well, tomorrow we should go see Mom and then I will take you out to eat. Then I suppose we should get on our way." Randy said, "I know it hasn't been fun, but I am going to miss you guys."

"Yah, but next time, let's go horseback riding on the farm!" Diane suggested.

"That's a deal!"

The light was blinking when they got back to their room. It was a message from Father Sebastian. "I think she would like to see you. Call me in the morning before you go over and I will be there. Call me at the rectory."

Diane's face fell, "I was almost hoping that he would say Mom didn't want to see us. I guess I need to grow up. I have to remember what Sebastian said about how she was probably calling him names in her head. I'm sure she has a few good ones for me."

They called their families and friends to say they would be leaving the next day and then went for a walk. Bea and Randy sat on the bench for a long talk. Matt and Diane walked down the hill and found a park that overlooked the ocean. They found a seat made out of stone and sat down to rest.

Matt put his arms around her and kissed her neck, "I want to get home as soon as we can. And in our little cabin, I want to make mad, passionate love to you."

"Are you going to have the pets in or out?"

"Mood zapper. That's my girl." Matt laughed. "Let's go back. We can hope that Randy and Bea are in bed and we can take the other room."

They got back and Randy and Bea were in bed, but not together. They kissed goodnight and went to their own rooms.

## 17

The next morning, they checked out and packed their cars. Then they arranged to meet with Father Sebastian for breakfast before they went to the hospital. Over breakfast, he said, "Your Mom was doing better last night and should be transferred to St. Jude's this afternoon. That is very promising."

"So, she may recover?" Bea asked.

"Doubtful. Fitz told me the doctors seem to think that between the crack to her head, the bout with meningitis and now the stroke; her fate is pretty much sealed. She does communicate, with blinks. One for yes, two for no and the dirty looks speak for themselves. She is a handful. She can let you know her displeasure with her eyes. I've never seen that so well done before," the priest shook his head. "Too bad she doesn't work that hard at being nice."

"My psychiatrist told me that I cannot move forward in my life until I make a stand with my mother. It should have been done years ago, but I was afraid. Still am. I've been rehearsing what I want to say, but I'm sure I won't get a word out. I never did before," Diane predicted.

"Remember, she can't interrupt you. You can say what you need to say."

"I don't know if it is proper to tell her how I feel now, when she can't say anything."

"It is her own fault she is in this situation. You have to do what you feel you should."

After breakfast, they drove over to the hospital. Father Sebastian went in to see her first, while the kids waited outside in the waiting room.

"Good morning, Loretta," he said. "I hope you slept well."

She looked at him and blinked once, but in her head, she was thinking:

*You damned fool, of course I slept! There's not another miserable thing to do. You sure took your time showing up. I can smell bacon on your breath! You are such a slovenly idiot.*

"Loretta," he smiled, "There is someone here to see you. Your children came today since they are leaving for their homes. They would like to tell you goodbye."

Her eyes snapped toward the priest, and he tried to read what that meant. "You said yesterday that you wanted to see them, remember?"

She stared.

"Okay, I'll tell them you don't, but are you certain? Think it over carefully, because you'll never get this chance again."

*I hate you, you miserable fool. What are we going to talk about? They don't love me and we all know it! This is just to calm their guilt. They deserve to feel guilty. Look what they did to me! If I could get up, I would crack them a good one.*

"Loretta," the priest took her limp hand, "Don't do this to yourself. You have caused yourself enough pain. Don't do it anymore. Think about it."

*What the hell do you know? I didn't cause my pain. They did! That miserable eunuch of a husband walked out on me and these kids sucked the lifeblood out of me. Now they are trying to blame their worthless lives on me.*

Father Sebastian grinned straight into her face, "I can see you screaming your head off with every filthy thing you can think to say, right now! Aren't you? Admit it!"

She stared a minute longer and then blinked once.

He chuckled, "I knew it. Knock it off. I know how tough you are, so you don't need to prove it to me. This is a favor you owe yourself. Remember what we talked about yesterday?"

She blinked once again.

"Okay, I will go ask Randy to come in. Can I count on you to behave?"

She glared at him.

He teased, "I heard that."

*You are such an ass! When I get out of here, I am going to make you regret the day you met me! Mark my words. You will have to pay dearly for every stupid remark you make, you imbecile.*

Sebastian motioned for Randy and then gave him a hug. "If you need me, I will be right here."

Randy nodded and went in. He was shocked when he saw how frail this woman who had caused him so much pain looked. The tears and anguish she had caused! Now she was trapped in her own puny body. He took a deep breath and went to the bed.

He touched her shoulder and said, "Hi Mom. It's Randy."

Her eyes moved toward him and he was sure she started to tear up. "Somewhere along the line, our relationship got all out of whack; but you're still my mom. I can't say that I approve of what you did, but I do want the best for you. I can't stand to think that you feel that I don't care. I wanted your love more than anything. It was never there. Maybe you couldn't help it, maybe I was unlovable, but regardless we both know that is the way it was. I hope you get well and find some kind of peace in this world. Mom, I wish it hadn't been this way."

Now he knew she was crying. He took a tissue and wiped her eyes. "I have to go back to work now. I want you to know that I am going to marry Bea. I will keep in touch with Father Sebastian. I won't be taking responsibility for any of your affairs. Mr. Fitz seems very proficient and can handle it. It is more convenient because he is here. Take care Mom."

Then he hugged her and wiped his tears. "I'm so sorry it had to end this way. It is unlikely I will see you again."

He walked briskly out of the room and went immediately to the rest room.

*I loved you, Randy! You didn't seem to understand that. I really did, but how could you love someone like me? I couldn't walk or anything.*

*You just never understood how much I counted on you. I don't want to you to leave. Why can't you stay with me? You are my son. My only son. You should be with me.*

Father Sebastian went in to Loretta. He wiped her tears and then said, "I will call in Diane now."

Loretta blinked twice. He stopped, "Do you want to see her?"

She blinked once and then looked at him, trying to convey something.

"Do you need a minute to regroup?"

She blinked once and then her face flooded with tears. He consoled her as best he could and after a few minutes, he said, "Let's call Diane. Okay?"

She blinked once.

The priest motioned for Diane and she came to the door. "How is she?" she whispered.

"She is very sad. She knows she will likely not see Randy again and it is her fault. That would not be a fun thing to face."

Diane nodded and then went in.

Inside the room, she found some strength deep inside herself and moved toward her mother. She took her Mom's hand, "Hi Mom."

Her Mom looked at her and the tears came again. Diane said, "Mom, I hope you will understand why I have to be out of your life. It isn't that I didn't want you in my life for years, but it always ended up being hurtful. I can't do that anymore. I really want to, but I just can't. Do you know, if you'd have been nicer to Matt and me, we would've brought you to North Dakota to be near us? We wanted to do that. But you couldn't even try to be nice. You tried to murder the man I love and you know what? He is a very kind man. You made a big mistake. I'm so sorry for what we have both missed. Our whole lives, when we could have shared the giggles, stories and adventures, you were always plotting to destroy any bit of happiness. Maybe you could have been in our weddings and held your grandchildren. You know, now we aren't even able trust you to be alone with anyone we love! I know this is not the time to bring up the loss of our father, but he was our father. We had the right to get to know him and share our lives. Everything ended up all a big mess. Everything was spoiled and ruined. There is nothing left anymore, Mom. I can't even try. I wish it could have been different, but I guess not. Be as strong as you can and my hope is that you can make the best of the rest of your life. Good bye, Mom."

Loretta was in shock. In her whole life, she had never heard her daughter say more than a few sentences before she collapsed in fear. She felt the tears and wanted so much for her daughter to hug her or something, but she didn't. Diane looked at her and then turned and walked away.

Diane went out the door and told Father Sebastian, "I don't think I was very nice to her. Should I have been?"

"I can't tell you that. You have to handle it the way you think. You've had to deal with her for years. Thank you for coming to see her. I want to go check on her and then maybe come out and talk to you all before you leave. Okay?"

"Sure. I'll tell them to wait. Is Randy okay?"

"Matt went to talk to him. Bea is over there."

The Father came back to see Loretta, "How are you doing?"

The tears gave him his answer. He held her as best he could and then wiped her tears. "Loretta, I'm going to tell them goodbye and then I'll come back in to sit with you for a while. Okay?"

She looked at him with that fear.

He smiled compassionately, "Don't worry, I'll be back. Trust me."

They all met on the patio and shared a word of prayer. "I know it has been a difficult thing for all concerned, but it needed to be done. I will try to work with her and see what we can do. I would like to be able to offer her hope."

"Whatever you think, but if she thinks that she can worm herself easily back into our lives, she won't realize what she's done," Randy said. "But use your judgment. I don't want to go through this ever again."

"Me, either," Diane said, and cried into Matt's shoulders.

"We'll keep in touch," Matt said. "And feel free to call."

"Yes," Randy said. "Please do."

On the way to their cars, the men decided to meet at the park by the beach to collect themselves before they got on the road. Once in the car, Diane said, "Matt, I was so cold-hearted, I couldn't believe it was me. I should have been nicer."

"Don't start that. Nothing is carved in stone. You can start a relationship with her again, but promise me you'll give it a little time. Let things settle for a while. Talk to Samuels about it. Okay? You have kept this bottled up for too long as it is. Of course, it would be cold-hearted now. It was held too long."

Diane looked at the passing traffic, "I know that is true. Honestly I do, but I felt so bad for her. I don't like to watch people suffer, even if they deserve it."

"I know. It is probably beneficial to her. If someone had been able to get her to listen long enough to be told off before, she might never got this deep in a mess. Trust the good Lord. He can fix anything if we give Him the chance."

"Yah. Guess this is as least as good as being in jail. If she had been successful, I would be almost a widow again."

Matt smiled, "I want you to be my wife first."

"Good idea," she smiled back.

After the four sat under a tree at a picnic table and drank some sodas, they hugged each other and said goodbye. "Call us tonight. We are going to be in Dover," Randy said. "Bea doesn't feel up to traveling to New Hampshire for Easter."

"We'll call when we get to Boston. Love you guys."

A few hours later, Matt and Diane were driving into a gorgeous day. The sun was bright and the grass was green. The sky was a pure deep blue. Matt reached over and squeezed her hand.

Meanwhile, Randy and Bea were following the coast toward Dover. "It is a glorious day, isn't it?" Bea said.

Randy pulled over on a seaside turnout. He stopped the car and went around to help her out. "It is wonderful. Bea, I need to tell you something. I want to promise you that I will do everything I can to help you have a good life. I love you so much. I know I won't always do right by you, but I want to."

"I know Randy. You are the most important person in the world to me. I thank God every day that I met you. Isn't it a beautiful day?"

"Yes, it really is."

# 18

The gurney moved down the hall and two burly men transferred a tiny patient to a hospital bed. A priest followed behind them. After they got her settled, the attendants left the dull green room.

Father Sebastian came up beside the lady, "It is a beautiful day. Would you like me to open the window to get some fresh air?"

She stared.

"I'll take that as a yes."

He moved over and after a few jerks got the window open. He then came over to the patient who was still staring blankly into space. "Loretta, what would you like to do? I can bring a book to read. Would you like that?"

No response.

"I can talk," he suggested.

He got a filthy look from her, "Okay Loretta, if you don't want me here, I can leave you alone. Would you prefer that?"

Nothing.

"I'm going for a walk. I want a cup of coffee. You can lay here alone. Enjoy yourself."

He walked out and she heard the door close. It was deathly quiet. She hated it. The only movement was the slight breeze from the window. She looked around as far as she could without her head moving. The ceiling was dirty and needed paint. The light fixture had a dead bug in it. Suddenly, she became furious.

*What the hell kind of a dump did they stick me in? For all I know, they took all my money and left me on welfare without a cent to my name. I hate them all. Who are those damned kids that they think they can walk out on me? Feeling so sorry for themselves! What a crock. They deserved all the trouble they ever got. They should have had it worse! Trying to pin it all on me! How dare they?*

*I wonder where that no-good priest is off too! He probably left me, too. Everyone does. I'll show them! I don't need any of them! They'll be sorry when I walk out of here! I will do it, too. Just wait. I'll pay them all back. Their requitement will make this last week look like playschool.*

*I think Sebastian should be coming back soon. He really wouldn't leave me, would he? He is a man of the cloth. They have to help people. That's their job! He doesn't do another damned thing all day.*

She heard a bump on the door, and it opened.

*That must be that priest. About time he came back!*

An attendant came in to put some things in her cupboard. The attendant never said anything to her and left the room. Suddenly, Loretta was frightened and very alone.

*Damn, it was only some skank with a washcloth and bedpan. Where the hell did that priest go? I will get him defrocked.*

Then she heard him come in, "Hi, look what I found! Someone had a copy of *Gone with the Wind*. I saw the movie but never read the book. How about you?"

He noticed she had tears in her eyes, and stopped. He became very serious, "Loretta, no matter how mean you get, I won't forget you. God never leaves His children. We can only leave Him."

She moved her eyes toward him and he smiled, "Now, shall we read this book?"

She blinked once.